Divine Madness

A Novel

Lynne Kaufman

TAILWINDS PRESS

Divine Madness, although inspired by real people and events, is a work of fiction. Where real-life historical figures appear, the situations, incidents, and dialogues concerning those persons are fictional and are not intended to depict actual events or to change the fictional nature of the work. In all other respects, any resemblance to actual persons, living or dead, events, or locales is entirely coincidental.

Copyright © 2022 by Lynne Kaufman. All rights reserved. Except as permitted under the U.S. Copyright Act of 1976, no part of this publication may be reproduced, distributed, or transmitted in any form or by any means, or stored in a database or retrieval system, without the written permission of the publisher.

Tailwinds Press
P.O. Box 2283, Radio City Station
New York, NY 10101-2283
www.tailwindspress.com

Published in the United States of America
ISBN: 979-8-9853124-0-9
1st ed. 2022

To those for whom writing is everything

If only one knew what to remember or pretend to remember. Make a decision and what you want from the lost things will present itself. You can take it down from the shelf like a can. Perhaps.

— Elizabeth Hardwick, *Sleepless Nights*

Once upon a time, a certain fairy tale goes, the most interesting and articulate minds in the world converged in dank Manhattan apartments to debate the merits of literature, ideas, and Trotskyist politics over cocktails.

— Michelle Dean, *The New Republic*

Divine Madness

CASTINE, MAINE: 1977

This is the first page of my manuscript, and I am not certain whether to call the narrator I or she. Either way it's me. I am writing this during the two weeks that Cal will be away, visiting Caroline and her daughters in Ireland. Cal says he will return to New York on September 15 and wants to move back in with me into our old apartment on 67th Street across from Central Park. It's where we lived for most of the twenty-one years of our marriage until he left me for Caroline. It's where I've lived for the past seven years without Cal. I've already mentioned Cal three times in this short space and Caroline twice and not yet named myself. It's a familiar pattern. I prefer writing about other people. I've never kept a diary. I write for publication.

However, in these pages, which I don't plan to show to anyone, I intend to overcome my reticence and reveal the details of my personal life without evasion or censure. Without trying to make myself look good. Without regard for writing correctly or well. I gain clarity through the process of writing. I need that clarity now.

When Cal was writing the poems that became *Life Studies* he felt blocked and asked me for help. He was trying to use metaphors and aliases in his reporting of a difficult time in his life. "Why not say what happened?" I suggested. I don't remember saying it. But he does. "You released my writer's block," he said. I was glad to be of help.

But when he turned that mantra against me in his defense of his scurrilous, scathing sonnet sequence, *The Dolphin*, I hated him. I have never been so hurt in my life, and I told him so. Of course, I told him many other things, too, loyal, loving, compassionate things.

I wrote, "I will be there whenever you want me, and not there whenever you don't." I need to explain that. It sounds docile, slavish. When we married in 1949, it could have been a common utterance by many a devoted wife. But I wrote it last year. Yes, wrote it. We mostly communicated by letters during those seven long years of separation. Trans-Atlantic phone calls were hideously expensive and the static unnerving. Sometimes other conversations overlapped with ours, and we weren't sure who was talking. During one of those fragmented exchanges Cal joked, "You're spending all your alimony on these phone calls." And we went back to writing letters.

Cal and I are people of the word. Style matters. Originality matters. Precision matters. Mark Twain got it right. "The difference between the right word and the almost right word is the difference between lightning and the lightning bug." Phillip Rahv, the editor of *The Partisan Review*, was even more explicit. "Writing is everything."

It is to us serious writers. "We don't get the news from poetry yet people die miserably every day for lack of what's found there." William Carlos William, medical doctor and renowned poet. He was one of the sane ones in our circle. One of the few who didn't jump off a building, or drink themselves to death, or spend months institutionalized.

Cal suffered from bipolar illness. In the twenty years of our marriage he was hospitalized annually. Usually in the winter. I could see it coming on. Hyper-excitability. Not sleeping. Heavy drinking. Writing nonstop. Impulsively inviting everyone he knew to a party at our house. Falling in love with a pretty young woman, a student, an acolyte, Lord knows there were enough of them.

Even now, battle-worn with a heart condition, he's a stunner. Tall, with that leonine head, unruly white hair tumbling down his forehead, that heartbreaking smile (with those small teeth just like Charlotte, his monstrous mother). His brilliant shambling talk. And the way he listened. He loved intelligent, articulate women. The wife before me and the wife after me were also writers.

In the grip of pre-mania, he would vow his love to each new "girl" and promise to marry her as soon as he divorced me. Interestingly, they all believed him, and after the mania and the depression when he reneged, they still held him in their affections. As he did them.

Did I know what I was getting into when I married Cal? Not really. Although his first manic episode happened shortly before our wedding. We had reconnected that summer at Yaddo, the arts colony in Saratoga Springs. Although we had met several times before at Philip Rahv's parties, Cal didn't remember me. And why should he? During those times he was shepherded by his wife, Jean Stafford, and basking in the fame of being Robert Lowell, the most influential poet in America. I, on the other hand, had published one scantly but respectfully reviewed novel and, on the basis of that, been asked by Rahv to write reviews for books and theatre. And, in a sense, that's what I still do. My reviews are more like essays, though. It's not a question of judging a literary work good or bad but of creating an engagement between the mind of the reviewer and the mind of the reader. It's about having something significant to say, which is why, I suppose, my highest praise was from Cynthia Ozick who said, *Her essays have plots.*

PARTISAN REVIEW

While still a girl trapped in Kentucky, I am an avid reader of the *Partisan Review* and long to write for it. I research its history, how it was launched in 1934 by William Phillips and Philip Rahv, funded by the John Reed Club of New York and affiliated with the Communist Party USA. And how shortly after the news of Stalin's purges was known, the *Review* became staunchly anti-Communist, though still remaining committed to new forms of art and radical politics.

My dream is to become a "Jewish intellectual." In truth, I am a lukewarm Protestant, but for me "Jewish intellectual" means urban, free-thinking, left-leaning. I encounter members of the tribe when I am getting my masters at Columbia University. I write to my mother that the smartest people in my class are the Jews, the ones she would call Hebrews.

I am living in a residential hotel in a platonic relationship with a homosexual jazz fanatic who takes me to

Harlem to see Billie Holiday and Louis Armstrong. I am a Manhattanite with late nights, alcohol, and clothes strewn on the floor.

I have a crush on Philip Rahv and sleep with him just as does Mary McCarthy and every other WASP who writes for him. He is short, swarthy, with a wrestler's build and dark brown eyes that never leave your face. He emigrated from Poland as a boy and never loses the guttural accent and rough manners which we women somehow find alluring. Sylvia Plath writes that at heart every woman loves a fascist. I hope it isn't true.

Ah, but the people Rahv publishes: Samuel Beckett, Franz Kafka, Alan Ginsburg, Jean-Paul Sartre, James Baldwin, Saul Bellow, George Orwell, Arthur Koestler, William Styron, Philip Roth.

Two of T.S. Eliot's "Four Quartets" appear first in PR. Who wouldn't want to be in that company?

YADDO

The summer after the *Partisan Review* party, I see Cal again at Yaddo. Without his wife and entourage, he is just another artist whiling away a summer at the Saratoga Springs colony. Its four hundred acres of pine groves, manicured lawns, rose gardens, and artificial lakes are a welcome retreat from the blistering asphalt of the city. The motto of Yaddo, "Supporting artists to work without interruption in a supportive environment," is honored during daylight, but when evening comes there is a communal dinner with abundant drink and subsequent carousing. Most of us are housed in the fifty-five room Tudor mansion, and doors are heard to open and close in a libidinal rhythm.

That first evening, I am seated next to Peter Taylor, which is unfortunate, as I've just reviewed his debut book of short stories and found it bland. He quotes my review back to me, very bad form. "A first book by a young author needs to take risks, to dare harshness, indiscretion, ugliness in a battle with the inexpressible. Peter Taylor does none of that." And stalks off.

The next night, Cal sits next to me and continues the attack. "You called my friend, Peter, 'corrigible.'"

This time I'm ready. "What's wrong with that?" I counter. "'Corrigible' means 'can be corrected or improved.' There's hope for him."

"He says you're a ball-breaker."

"He needs stronger balls."

"I like your style." Cal downs his soup. "First time here?"

I nod yes; then in his Boston Brahmin accent he discourses on the history and folklore of the place. It was built by the financier Spenser Trask as a family home, but when all four of his offspring died in childhood, Trask converted the mansion to an artists' colony for his grieving wife. She named it Yaddo, in memory of the youngest child's mispronunciation of "shadow." Cal gestures towards the nets that hang on the dining room wall. "Do you know what those are for?"

As if on cue, the answer comes bursting into the room. A bat frantically flying figure eights across the ceiling. As the guests weave and duck, Peter Taylor, in a skillful maneuver using two nets, captures the intruder and releases it unharmed into the night. Peter returns to a round of applause. "When it comes to bats, that man has balls," Cal says. I smile at the rejoinder, and he stands and pulls out my chair. "Come and join me for a smoke." He places his hand on my lower back. I feel the tingle of his palm through the thin cloth of my dress. He keeps his hand there as we tour the garden. The scent of the fully blown roses adds to the headiness.

"Behold the sundial," he says as he reads its inscription aloud.

"Hours fly, flowers die. New days, new ways, pass by. Love stays."

"Consider that foreplay," he says, drawing me towards him. "Let's use your room, mine is a disaster." I later learn that every room Cal stays in becomes a disaster. He is consummately messy. Cigarette butts, discarded clothing, crumpled papers, piles of books, half-eaten meals are everywhere.

My room is neat as a nun's cell. He shrugs his clothes off and onto the floor. I fold mine and place them in the dresser drawer. We are in no hurry, contrary to the frenzied first mating dance choreographed in the movies, with wall-banging, brutal kisses, torn shirts. Our lovemaking is measured and decorous. He strokes my body, flat stomach, rounded breasts and ass. A perfect handful, he declaims. I'm equally pleased with Cal's body, lean and muscular, with a broad and downy chest. He is well endowed and already priapic. He doesn't need any further stimulation from me, although I am ready to offer it. Instead we assume the missionary position. He thrusts hard. I match his rhythm as I rub my clitoris. He ejaculates, and in due time I come too.

As the evening air cools our sweat-soaked skin, he lights my cigarette with his own. Our filmic moment. We inhale deeply, curl up against each other, and talk for hours. The talk is far more lasting, varied, and thrilling than the sex. I am in love with his mind. The mind that creates the brilliant poems I devour. I devour him, too, before morning, showing my lingual skills. I am far from being a virgin, having lived as a single woman in a hotel room in New York City for ten years. Now, at thirty-three, I've had many lovers. It's been both liberating and a good way to advance my career.

But none of them mattered. From now on, it's only Cal. Time for me to settle down. A first marriage for me. A second for Cal. Jean Stafford won't be too surprised. In our literary set, lovers circle around like a game of musical chairs.

On this round, though, I emerge victorious as I become Mrs. Robert Lowell. He has already won the Pulitzer for *Lord Weary's Castle* last year, at the age of thirty, and followed that with multiple grants and honors and an offer of a teaching post at the University of Iowa. He is well on his way to becoming America's foremost poet.

My friend, Mary McCarthy, warns me about reports of Cal's violent behavior. Do you know how he got the nickname "Cal"? Cal for Caligula, the cruel and deranged

Divine Madness

Roman emperor. Cal for Caliban, the spawn of a monster. He was a bully in prep school, knocked his father down in an argument. He broke Jean Stafford's nose twice, once by crashing his car while drunk and another in a domestic brawl fueled by alcohol. But Jean suffers from mental instability and alcoholism, and I do not.

Cal and I spend most of the month at Yaddo in my bedroom. The two studios delegated to us wind up as storage closets for Cal's overflow of papers, books and soiled clothing. I keep "our" room fresh and orderly. Our mornings start late, when Cal goes down to the kitchen and brings up thermoses filled with enough strong coffee to keep us going until bourbon time. He sprawls out on our bed and stays there all day writing feverishly, crossing out lines with such force that it tears the page.

When he is pleased with a verse, he shouts, "Lizzie." I am sitting across the room typing away. If I don't look up immediately, he rolls off the bed, covers the space between us in two strides and grasps my shoulders. "Listen," he commands as he reads the newly composed verse. I listen and tell him it's good. And it is. "But what about this?" he cries. And then he reads several variations, some altering a word or two, some radically different. "Which one?" he demands.

"Let me read them." I reach for the sheet of paper, but he evades me. "Poetry is music. It has to be heard." He then proceeds to read each version in turn, gauging my expression, pausing for my comments. It isn't that strange; many poets I've met hold court at any public opportunity to declaim their verses. Unlike most prose writers, poets are truly possessed by language. It seems to be barreling through their brains, ready to roll off their tongues at every moment. And, among the best of them, it colors and shapes their everyday speech. Poets live in metaphor. They see a different world. Just as dogs hear sounds we can't hear and perceive odors we can't detect. Poets are a different species. No wonder, however messy and difficult they are, poets are never at a shortage for adoring women to organize their lives.

I know that. And yet, when I go down to the communal laundry, I take his soiled shirts, shorts, socks, and yes, his underwear. I'm running the machines for my own clothes, I reason, so why stand on ceremony? He's inept, and I can do it easily. I believe I can run a house and write. I believe I can wear make-up and high heels and silk dresses and still be smart and snippy and independent.

But don't tell me men and women are equal. That will never happen as long as men are physically stronger. Any woman who has had her wrist twisted by a man will ascertain that. I have not been the recipient of violence, but I am aware of it. Mary tells me I get away with murder because I play the Southern belle. I argue that I've lost my Southern drawl, but when I hear my voice recorded, it's clear that I haven't. I'm blonde and small-boned, five foot

Divine Madness

two, but I hold my own. Some say I have an acid tongue. Not that I show that to Cal. Why would I? He evokes tenderness, caring, admiration. I am in love.

MANIA

I leave Yaddo reluctantly. I have to return to the *Review*. Cal has another month to work on his poetry cycle. It is about his New England ancestors. We part in a tearful farewell. I promise to drive back in two weeks. He promises to write to me.

I miss him terribly. It feels as if a limb has been amputated. And then I get a telephone call from Elizabeth Bishop. She is one of Cal's closest friends. They write each other frequent, long, and eloquent letters, sharing their poetry, their most private thoughts. They've fallen in love with each other off and on for years. Cal has proposed marriage and she would have accepted if she wasn't a lesbian.

Elizabeth tells me that during the last week Cal has displayed signs of increased mania. In the past he has been able to ward off what might become a full-blown attack by an immediate voluntary hospitalization. This time, since he is at Yaddo, no one intervenes. The other guests observe his increasingly bizarre behavior with bemusement. Theatricality is not uncommon with poets. So his loud volume, his haunted eyes, his buttonholing the nearest listeners seem a reenactment, a parody of "The Ancient Mariner." But when he starts falling down drunk, smashing crockery, brandishing a cleaver, the director of Yaddo calls the police.

When they arrive, he resists strenuously, Elizabeth tells me. It takes four men to restrain him. He is brought to the nearest hospital in a straitjacket. Elizabeth has spoken to his regular doctor. He is placed in a padded cell, given Thorazine. When the mania abates, he will begin a regimen of daily walks, hydrotherapy, and psychiatric sessions. Although Elizabeth declares the psychiatric sessions are as useful to his condition as they would be for a broken leg. The fits come upon him, she explains, and they need to run their course. Afterwards he is morose, repentant and deeply ashamed. Then the depression lifts, and he is his old wonderful self again. It's deeply disturbing, but there's nothing you can do about it. Consider it tornado season. If I were you, she advises, I'd stay clear of it.

I drive to McLean Hospital the following week. It is the earliest Cal is allowed visitors. I am bringing, at his request, a boxful of books: Shakespeare, Dante, and T.S. Eliot, six yellow legal pads and a handful of pencils and pens. He is slowly coming down from the heights of the mania but still has its creative fervor. He is writing nonstop, although when he shows me page after page of his poems they make little sense to me. I try to cover my confusion, but he picks it up immediately. "Lizzie, don't spare my feelings. It makes me furious when I think people are hiding things from me. It stokes my paranoia." He tears open the pack of cigarettes I've brought. His hands tremble; he can't strike the match. I do it for him, take the cigarette between my own lips and light it. As I pass it to him, it recalls a flash of our post-coital smoking. I feel an erotic stir and take his hand. He lifts my palm, presses it against his cheek and holds it there. "I know the poems are chaos now," he says, "but in time, I'll decipher them. Break the code. Find the gold."

"It's time for Professor's treatment," a pretty nurse says as she enters the room. Cal greets her with his native courtliness. "My angel of mercy." She helps him to stand and settles him into the waiting wheelchair. He reaches back to his bed for the cigarettes. "Now, now, Professor," his angel chides. Cal flashes a dazzling smile. "I can't start any fires in the bathtub," he says as he tucks the pack and the book of matches in his pajama top pocket. The angel shrugs indulgently and wheels him out.

I stand there until the head nurse enters to see me out. I must look dazed. "First time here?" she asks. I nod. "Well, if you're going to go crazy, this is the place to do it," she says.

"It does look a lot like a country club," I say. "With

the most elite clientele," she offers. "You know what they say, if you're a true Bostonian, you have a membership in the Atheneum, a gravesite in Mount Auburn and a relative in McLean."

"What's the Atheneum?" I ask. "A private library," she answers, "membership only."

As I leave, I wonder if Cal's membership extends to me.

CAL WRITES TO ME FROM MCLEAN

"How would you care to be engaged? Like a debutante? WILL YOU?

"How happy we'll be together writing the world's masterpieces, swimming and washing dishes.

"P.S. Reading *The Idiot* again."

MARRIAGE

Cal leaves McLean, and at his urging, Jean Stafford gets a quickie divorce in Mexico. Two weeks later Cal and I are married at the Episcopal Church in Boston. "Will you, Elizabeth Hardwick, take Robert Trail Spence Lowell IV for your lawfully wedded husband?" It's the first time I've heard Cal's full lineage. The Lowells have been christened, married, and laid to rest for generations in this church. The only three times a Boston Brahmin should have his name in the newspaper, according to Cal's mother, Charlotte. The wedding is small, attended by Cal's parents, his beloved cousin Harriet, and Mary McCarthy, who lends me her Balenciaga for the ceremony. Mary also warns me about Charlotte, whom my predecessor, Jean, has dubbed Charlotte Hideous, a neurotic of very little brain.

Charlotte holds court at the celebratory lunch that afternoon. She regales me with stories about Bobby, as she calls her son, to differentiate him from her husband, Robert. "He was a sweet boy," she says, "and we were very close. He had a set of soldiers and we would set up all the battles that Napoleon fought and reenact them on the drawing room rug. Bobby has a formidable memory. He could tell you the place and date of every battle. Isn't that a fact, Bobby?" Cal gives her a thin smile and rattles off a few to her polite applause.

"It's the only thing I've ever done that's gotten your approval, right, Mother?" Charlotte brushes away the remark with a white-gloved hand. "It's never too late, Bobby." After his father pays the bill, he takes me aside. "I hope you know what you've gotten yourself into. From now on, he's your responsibility."

When I repeat that remark to Cal later that evening, in bed, as we share a bottle of champagne, he responds with surprise. "Really, that's the most gumption that old fool has ever shown." He proceeds to give me a rundown on his parents' marriage. "Charlotte Winslow, a member of the upper class and a dreadful social snob, married Robert Lowell for his name and for his money. To her disappointment, the money had long been squandered, but the name remained good social capital. Big Robert, as she sometimes called him, was a Navy officer when they met, but Charlotte didn't like following him on his assignments. She was rooted to Boston, to her social circle, her indolent friends. So she insisted he leave the Navy, a place where he was respected and competent, to take a position in a brokerage firm, for which he was ill suited and unsuccessful.

"She broke his spirit, just as she tried to break mine, by constant criticism. They took me to a psychiatrist when I was eight because I was doing badly in school, getting into fights, rebelling. I was sent away to boarding school where I continued all the same behaviors. But, among my peers, I was lionized. I was bigger and stronger and rowdier than the other boys. I caused more damage. I never lived at home again."

Cal refills our champagne glasses. "What about you?" he asks. "Why weren't your family at the wedding?" "Too far," I say, "and anyway, there are too many of them. I'm the ninth of eleven children. Lower-middle class. Lexington, Kentucky. Daddy ran a heating-plumbing service and Mama made pregnancy a full-time job."

"You're one of eleven," Cal says, "and I am one of one. Even so, Charlotte never wanted me. When she was pregnant she tried to kill herself."

"How do you know that?"

"She told me. Several times."

Knowing you are an unwanted child, do we ever get over that?

TELL ME EVERYTHING

Cal asks about my first sexual experience:
　I and several girls from the neighborhood met a very nice-looking old man with a kind and courtly smile. On Saturday afternoons he paid our way into the movies and bought us chocolate. In the dark with a little girl on each side, he ran his hand up our thighs. It was my first incidence of bribery. It grows like molars.

Cal asks about Kentucky:
　In the summer there were the evangelical tent meetings. There it was possible to be saved again and again. "Yes I take Jesus Christ as my personal savior." Lots of saved ones, weaving up to the front, have just come out of the penitentiary.

Lexington, the Bluegrass, Man o' War with his large melancholy skull on view. Horses everywhere and the wrinkled, broken jockeys with faces like walnut shells.

When I left home my brother said, "It will be wonderful if you make a success of life: then you can follow the races."

THE FIRST SEVEN YEARS

For seven years Cal and I move around a lot. Seven is a portentous number.

Genesis 41. Pharaoh dreamed that he was standing by the Nile and behold, there came out of the Nile seven cows, attractive and plump, and they fed in the reed grass. And behold, seven other cows, ugly and thin, came up out of the Nile after them and devoured the seven attractive and plump cows. And Pharaoh awoke.

And he fell asleep and dreamed a second time. And behold, seven ears of grain, plump and good, were growing on one stalk. And behold, after them sprouted seven ears, thin and blighted. And the thin ears swallowed up the seven plump ears. So in the morning Pharaoh's spirit was troubled and he sent for all the magicians of Egypt and all its wise men, but none could interpret his dreams.

Then the chief cupbearer remembered Joseph and

brought him from the dungeon. Joseph came before Pharaoh and told him that his dream meant there would be seven years of abundance in the land followed by seven years of famine. He recommended that a discerning and wise man be put in charge and that food should be collected in the good years and stored for use during the famine.

Pharaoh thought that was a good idea and gave Joseph the job. Is that how I got the job taking care of the Kingdom of Cal? By being practical? Joseph attributed his revelation to God. I did not.

For Cal and me, in our first seven years the lean and fat are intermingled. We travel in Europe. Live in Iowa. Live in Boston. In New York. We enjoy Europe. Paris is my favorite. Gloomy Amsterdam is Cal's. I find Iowa deadly dull, a throw-back to boring Lexington, Kentucky. Cal enjoys the adoration of his students. His lectures are freewheeling, and I mark his students' papers. Boston is prim and dusty and too close to his mother. It is odd that since this is his city, we do not seem to belong here. Thirty-six is neither young enough or old enough for certain places, but perhaps this city will interest him as it did when he was young. Now a lot of people seem to think he's an anarchist and he does often have the preoccupied look of a secret agent.

Just as always he reads and writes all day, here in this

house on the top floor, drinks quarts of milk, smokes cigarettes. He hates for me to play my jazz records, but sometimes I do late at night and then he dances like a bear.

His health? There's a sweet little psychiatrist here used to treating Boston women who have stayed too long at home and young men not doing well at the bank. He seems to think Cal is similar. The only thing that distresses the doctor, makes him look at his watch, is Cal's long "free associations" about Goethe. At the end of the session, he asks me if Goethe is a family friend?

We move to Manhattan which suits us well. With Cal's trust fund, we buy a spacious apartment on the west side overlooking Central Park and two nearby writing studios.

And each winter, wherever we are, Cal suffers another attack. He is diagnosed with multiple labels, schizophrenia, anxiety disorder, but most often manic-depressive. Thorazine calms the heights of his craziness but makes him a zombie.

His doctor recommends shock treatment. It is a medically induced epileptic fit that somehow scrambles the wiring of the brain sufficiently to stop the mania and return the patient to normal functioning. Sometimes it takes more than twenty treatments to bring about the desired result. The fatigue it causes and the memory loss are not calculated. It varies with each patient. Cal is young and strong.

Cal tells me about the procedure. He is wheeled in on

a gurney, his arms and legs strapped down. Graphite salve is applied to his temples, and the electrodes are attached. They place a piece of rubber hose between his teeth so he doesn't sever his tongue during the induced convulsions. They turn on the machine and release the current that passes through two layers of skin and bone and enters his brain. It lasts for two minutes and the power is from 70 to 150 volts, equivalent to lighting one large light bulb. It leaves a sparky smell of burning, corrosion, and battery acid. He is wheeled back to his room and sleeps for the rest of the day. There is a period when he feels dazed, foggy and weak; then he recovers. He is depressed, remorseful. That mood lifts. And we return to normal life until the next time.

I ask his doctor how ECT works. Electroconvulsive Therapy. When we call something by its initials, it seems less alien, less threatening. So ECT it will be. Although no one knows quite how or why it works, it seems to unsettle the brain patterns that were causing psychopathic behavior and allow healthier ones to take its place.

CREATIVITY AND MADNESS

I read every medical text I can find on manic depression and wind up gaining the most understanding through literature, emulating Nietzsche who declared that Dostoyevsky was the only psychologist he could learn something from.

I begin with Plato:

"The composers of lyrical poetry create those admired songs of theirs in a state of divine insanity. Madness, provided that it comes as a gift of heaven, is a channel by which we receive the greatest blessings."

How can you tell if the gift is from Heaven or Hell?

On to Kierkegaard:

"The poet is an unhappy man who in his heart harbors a deep anguish. His fate is like the unfortunate victims whom the tyrant Phalaris imprisoned in a brazen bull, and slowly tortured over a steady fire; their cries could not reach the tyrant's ears; when he heard them they sounded like sweet music."

What an apt image. All the suffering to create the art

is transformed when it reaches the audience's ears.

Back to Nietzsche:

"Artistic greatness can be earned only by suffering. To make oneself sick, mad, to provoke the symptoms of derangement gives him the power to see and tell the truth, and his suffering is repaid with insight."

Welcome the suffering. It is the price of great art.

Rimbaud.

"I call for an artificially induced deliberate derangement of all the senses. This would transform the tormented, self-sacrificial, even insane poet into 'the great invalid', 'the great criminal', 'the great accursed' and plunge him into unknown, unheard of, unnamable spiritual visions."

If madness doesn't come naturally, seek it.

Sartre on Rimbaud.

"In relation to Gauguin, van Gogh and Rimbaud, I have a distinct inferiority complex because they managed to destroy themselves. In order to achieve authenticity, something has to snap."

Sartre took mescaline and hallucinated being followed by crabs for a year.

What am I looking for in my research? An explanation? A justification? What I find is a benediction. Amor fati.

Divine Madness

Love your fate. Robert Lowell, the best lyric poet of his generation, is a genius and a madman. He is the only husband I will ever want. But for himself, he writes . . .

"The thin-skinned poet, who sees too much and feels too deeply, can never be contented."

THE NEXT SEVEN YEARS

We are both forty and although have no desire to change our way of living, the discovery that I am pregnant elates us. My first few months are rough and, because of that, Cal says we have become "timid, delicate and ante-bellum." We stay in Boston all summer on doctor's orders not because there are problems but because, says the doctor, we are too old to try again.

The baby isn't due until January, but by September we are already so exhausted that we lie around on sofas all day subsisting on cornflakes, no-calorie ginger ale and yogurt. I never move except to turn the pages of a newspaper, and Cal never moves except to change the records on the turntable.

Each day we notice little changes and stirrings. How strange to feel autumn coming on and knowing that almost before the year is out we will have a child. Cal says it's as though one were at last invited indoors after having slept outside on the ground all one's life.

Lynne Kaufman

We worry some about our child's health. Cal's manic depression is hereditary. There is a long line of ancestors including his mother who have been diagnosed with mental disorders, but we decide that my family's stable, although undistinguished genes will balance that.

OUR DAUGHTER

Harriet Winslow Lowell is born. She is a healthy and contented baby with my fair skin and Cal's sideways smile. We hire an Irish nanny, whose formidable competence intimidates us mightily, and Cal and I return to writing and teaching. He commutes to Harvard. I teach at Barnard. Cal is beguiled with Harriet, delights in her existence. It is as if up to now, he says, he's been lacking some prime faculty . . . like eyesight, hearing, reason. He is in domestic rhapsody, living on the moon with a creature as simple as primordial matter.

I do the day to day parenting: the meals, bath and bedtime rituals. And later make the appointments: doctor, dentist, play dates, nursery school. I love doing it. I remember reading once that when you have a child you make an agreement to have your heart walking around outside your body. Harriet and Cal are my world. And much later when Cal goes through one of his episodes, she is a great comfort and stabilizer for me. We wait together for his return, to become a family once again.

I have an indelible image. The first day we brought Harriet home, all three of us exhausted, Cal lay face up on our wide green sofa, I lay face up upon him, and upon my breast, wrapped in a pink blanket lay Harriet. We were complete.

THE *NEW YORK REVIEW OF BOOKS*

I write an essay for *Harpers*, "The Decline of Book Reviewing," that creates a great stir. Although the fates of authors and publishers depend on book reviews, no one has thought of reviewing the reviewers. So it's a first, and I don't spare any feelings. Not even the august *New York Times* or *Herald Tribune* escape my scorn. I call the reading of the Sunday morning book reviews a dismal experience, a mush of concession. Sweet, bland praise. A universal, lobotomized accommodation. And I go on . . .

"Books are now born in a puddle of treacle. Every author has 'filled a need,' is 'thanked for their contribution,' and excused for 'minor faults in an otherwise excellent work.' In fact the condition of positive reviewing has become so predictable that the publishers of *Lolita* have tried to stimulate sales by quoting the rare negative review.

"'*Lolita* is undeniably news in the world of books. Unfortunately it is bad news.'" Orville Prescott.

"'I am sorry that *Lolita* was ever published. I am sorry it was ever written.'" Gilbert Highet.

"Simple coverage seems to have won out over the drama of opinion. Readability has taken the place of good clear prose, which is a very different thing.

"The English papers, notably the *Times Literary Supplement*, set a standard much higher than our own newspapers. It is not just what they choose to review but the seriousness, the tone and the independence of mind of the reviewer. In England reviewing is an honorable form of writing. Capacious and thoughtful. Wide-ranging. We read them not for a quick, superficial judgment but to find out what an unusual mind, capable of presenting fresh ideas in a vivid and original manner, thinks of the book.

"This is why we need a great metropolitan publication that reviews the unusual, the difficult, the intransigent and above all, the interesting. Create one and it will find its audience."

Several years later, during the four-month-long newspaper strike, Cal and I and Barbara and Robert Silvers create one: the *New York Review of Books*.

Cal gets a loan on his trust fund, we invite our friends to contribute, and we map out the first issue on our dining room table. We state our mission as producing a new kind of magazine in which the most interesting and qualified minds of our times discuss current literature, arts, and politics in depth. Our first issue sells out its printing of

Divine Madness

100,000 copies, and we receive over 1,000 letters to the editor asking us to continue. And so we do, continue and thrive until every writer and thinker worth their intellectual heft wants to add the *New York Review of Books* to their resume.

For me, it becomes a literary home. It's where I publish many of the essays on women and writing that will later become *Seduction and Betrayal*. And I am in excellent company. It is where W.H. Auden, Robert Penn Warren, John Updike, Philip Roth, Lillian Hellman, Truman Capote, Saul Bellow, and Susan Sontag can be found. It is also where:

Ralph Nader publishes his manifesto for consumer justice

I.F. Stone investigates the lies of Watergate

Hannah Arendt reflects on the nature of evil

Mary McCarthy reports from Saigon on the Vietnam War

McGeorge Bundy outlines the nuclear threat

Desmond Tutu reports on the conflict over apartheid

Vaclav Havel writes from the Czech underground

Mark Danner reports on torture from the CIA black sites

And the most highbrow personal ads to be found anywhere.

Antediluvian Mariner (M) seeks attractive coxswain (F) to put in terra firma amidst coming torrents. Long-term relationship inevitable. Will steer clear of Mount Ararat in protest of Armenian genocide. Mont Blanc? Open to suggestions.

Or this one:

Worn out husband, friend of wife's nerves, father to 5 silly daughters (the 2 eldest excepted) for almost a quarter century seeks wealthy, titled, childless widow of an unentaled estate for long walks across ha-has.

None of us could find a meaning for *unentaled*. The closest we could come was a synonym for *un-entangled*. But we let it stand for a laugh. It wasn't until Caroline's usurpation that the impact of "wealthy, titled" took on import for me, as did the double meaning of "ha-has."

CAL PROTESTS WAR

Well before I knew him, Cal was a conscientious objector in World War 2. Rather than report to his draft board and register as a CO, he wrote a letter to President Franklin Roosevelt. "I no longer think war is justified. Furthermore, America is attempting to form another kind of totalitarian civil authority to substitute for the dictator regimes in Germany and Italy. I also strongly object to the mass bombings of German cities."

He was given a one-year prison sentence served first in a New York City jail, then the federal penitentiary in Danbury, Connecticut.

There he met Louis Lepke Bukalter, the head of the Kosher Nostra, the Mafia hit squad called Murder Inc.

Lepke to Cal, "I'm in for killing. What are you in for?"

Cal to Lepke: "I'm in for not killing."

Cal could have avoided the whole incident as he was eventually classified as 4F for bad eyesight. But having served his prison sentence was a badge of honor when he protested the War in Vietnam.

President Johnson, hoping to improve his administration's image, invited Cal to a White House Festival of the Arts. Cal accepted, then changed his mind. He wrote a letter to Johnson and sent a copy to the *New York Times,* which published it on the front page.

"We are in danger of becoming an explosive and suddenly chauvinistic nation and may even be drifting on our way to the last nuclear ruin. I feel I am serving you and our country best by not taking part in the White House Festival."

Twenty writers and artists supported him, including our friends Mary McCarthy, Hannah Arendt, and Robert Penn Warren.

Johnson screamed they were sons of bitches, fools, treasonous.

The following year, Yale University got a $25,000 grant from the NEA to produce Cal's translation of Aeschylus' *Prometheus Bound.* Johnson demanded the award be withdrawn. To his credit, Roger Stevens, the Chair of the NEA, refused. Our crowd went to opening night cheering the symbolism of LBJ as Zeus and Cal as Prometheus.

THE SEVEN YEARS AFTER THAT

Cal is invited to give a lecture in Buenos Aires. Harriet, who is now a manageable five, and I accompany him. The conference is sponsored by the Congress for Cultural Freedom, an anti-Communist organization secretly funded by the CIA. Cal is supposed to provide an ideological balance for the other major speaker, the Chilean communist poet Pablo Neruda. Although Cal is vehemently anti-Communist, he is also a great fan of Neruda. I wonder which sentiment will win. But I never have a chance to find out.

Before we travel to Argentina, we stop off in Brazil to see Elizabeth Bishop. Cal meets and immediately declares his love for a beautiful Brazilian novelist, whose stories Elizabeth has translated into English. The novelist admires his work but is not interested in him sexually. He then turns his attentions to Elizabeth Bishop and tries to induce her to marry him. She turns him down yet again. She is in love with a Brazilian woman, a flamboyant architect.

Cal mopes around like a lovesick teenager, ignoring me and Harriet. When he turns verbally abusive, even though I suspect this is mania brewing, I take the next plane back to New York. I enroll Harriet in day camp, start a series of articles on literary women, and put Cal's best friend, Blair Clark, on notice.

Cal flies to Buenos Aires, and soon there are scandals circulating at the American Embassy. He is drinking heavily, arriving hours late for appointments, and insulting important officials. That behavior escalates to declaring himself the Caesar of Argentina, taking off his clothes and climbing several equestrian statues. Although he frightens most of the women he encounters, he manages to have a few one-night stands. After a wild party, he locks himself in his hotel room with a woman who has agreed to calm him down, although she is now shouting that he is assaulting her. The manager arrives with several burly policemen who break down the door and tie him into a straitjacket.

Blair Clark flies down to Buenos Aires and takes Cal back to New York. Blair tells me that by the time the plane reaches its first stop, Cal has fallen in love with the stewardess. She manages to elude him and his offer to marry her and begin a "vida nueva" in some remote fastness of South America.

How do I stand it? How do I put up with it time and time again? Friends and non-friends have their theories. I am a masochist. I am a damaged enabler. I am a saint. I

Divine Madness

am doing penance for my bad karma. I am a control freak. I need to be needed.

It has been reported to me that Mary McCarthy said, "It would be better to let him be crazy once a year, be locked up, emerge penitent etc. than to have him subdued by drugs in a sort of private zoo, his home with Lizzie as his keeper. But Lizzie prefers it that way. She enjoys the power she has over Cal when he is sick, drugged and weak."

CAL WRITES ABOUT HIS ILLNESS TO HELP ME UNDERSTAND

There is no cure for mania, only remissions.

The electric shocks make me despair, take my memory away, numb my thinking, and my heart, make me absent, and aware of myself being absent. I see myself pursuing my own existence for weeks, like a dead man at the side of a living man who is no longer himself. I fear that the next time I may not recover or the part of my brain used for poetry will be burned away.

When mad, I have no conscience, when sane, I am guilt-stricken and ashamed.
    I emerge low as dirt, suffering from the memories of how I have caused such hurt to people I love. Then extreme depression, aching, self-enclosed, fearful of everyone and everything anyone can do, feeling I am nothing and can do nothing.

By the time I reach the hospital, I am completely out of my head. I can smell the sulfur on my pajamas. I am emanating the brimstone of Hell. I am a prophet and everything is a symbol.

Then in the hospital, shouting, singing, tearing things up . . . religious ravings, clownish antics.

In my dreams I am like one of Michelangelo's bulky, rugged statues that can be tumbled down a hill without injury. But when I wake, it's as though I've been flayed, each nerve beaten with a rubber hose.

I've been brought down to my knees sixteen times. I got up sixteen times. But one day if I don't get up, I don't mind.

I have such a fear of permanent madness. Christ, may I die at night with a semblance of my faculties.

BIPOLAR

Over the years, Cal is confined in five different countries and in fifteen psychiatric hospitals and clinics. He compares his hermetic existence in the asylums to the self-enclosed life of boarding schools, writers' colonies and prison, all of which he has experienced. After William Carlos Williams had his own nervous breakdown, Cal counseled him, "We patients all think it's better on the outside but agree that we're lucky to have such a place when we need it."

When I remind him of Winston Churchill's saying, while suffering a bout of his famous Black Dog depression, "We are all worms," Cal finishes, "but I do believe I am a glow-worm."

Remarkable breakdown. Remarkable recovery. That's my remarkable Cal.

HOSPITALS WHERE CAL WAS CONFINED AND I VISITED HIM

Baldpate, Georgetown, Massachusetts
Payne Whitney, New York City
U.S, Military Hospital, Munich
Kreuzlinger, Switzerland
Jewish Hospital, Cincinnati
Massachusetts Mental Hospital, Boston
McLean, Belmont, Massachusetts
Columbia Presbyterian, New York City
Clinica Bethlehem, Buenos Aires
Institute of Living, Hartford, Connecticut
Greenways, Primrose Hill, London
The Priory, Roehampton, London
St. Andrews, Northampton, England
Massachusetts General, Boston

THE TWENTY-FIRST YEAR

Cal receives an invitation for a six-week residency at All Souls College at Oxford University. It is a dream assignment for scholars and writers. It has no students. Therefore, no classes to teach. No meetings to attend. Only forty like-minded men living in spacious quarters in historic buildings, having the services of a "scout" to do laundry and housekeeping, provided with all meals including evening High Table, where one is offered vintage wine and erudite conversation. No distracting women or children. Uninterrupted time for reading, writing and thinking.

I am somewhat concerned about being separated from Cal for that long, but we decide to take a family vacation the month before. We will show Harriet Italy. Then she and I will return to New York; Cal will go on to Oxford and return to us in June.

And then the very next week, another offer arrives, a two-year appointment from Essex College, a new university an hour's train line from London. Cal is ecstatic. He takes it as a sign. We are meant to leave America, to take a sabbatical. Both of us are opposed to the current administration and the Vietnam War. Indeed, we recently marched against the bombing of Cambodia. London is our favorite city with theatre, concerts and lectures galore. Lots of literary friends. Harriet could attend an excellent school that would broaden her horizons. Trips on the Continent during school breaks. And to sweeten the pot, Cal declares . . . "And. Lizzie darling, you can take the year off from Barnard and do nothing but write."

He is so keen to go that it is hard for me to resist. I agree but modify the stay to one year. He calls Harvard, requests a leave of absence and wires Essex his delighted acceptance. The rest is up to me. I sublet our apartment and our studios, find a home for the car and for Sumner the cat, set up a banking account in London, and pack our suitcases. We set off for Italy: Venice, Florence and Rome. Harriet discovers a passion for Renaissance art and rum raisin gelato. We part from Cal at the Rome Airport, with long goodbyes. He promises to write every day, as do I.

And he does for the first week. He describes the grassy quad, the meandering Thames, the ancient pubs and bookshops. He draws caricatures of some of the more eccentric Oxford dons for Harriet and tells of how lonely he is without us. He is going to London next weekend to attend a party his publisher, Faber and Faber, is having in his honor. After spending so much time in monkish isolation, he writes, he is looking forward to being reintroduced to the feminine.

I answer each letter, hoping he is having a wonderful and productive time, and apologizing for the questions about boring household details, but we have gotten a request from Stony Brook University for his archives. Shall I accept it? He writes back that he prefers Harvard. Can I organize the material and get both bids? Not without him, I reply. What to make public? What to keep private? What to seal until both of us are gone?

Use your best judgment, he says as he always does where there are decisions that need organization. So I do, reserving the thorniest revelations (love letters from his many affairs, correspondence that shows prejudice and slander) for his reckoning when he returns in June.

Although our letters keep up the pretense of daily conversation about Harriet and the household and our plans for moving to England, he is evasive. Instead he talks about the political events unfolding, the U.S. bombing of Cambodia, the Black Panther trial, the killing of the students at Kent State. Something is wrong between us and I am afraid to ask.

Then the letters stop. No phone calls. No telegrams. Silence for a week. Then two. Then three. I continue to write to him every day. Growing more concerned. More agitated. I need to know if he's found a place for us to live in London. Has he found a school for Harriet? Finally, I call All Souls College and learn from the porter than Cal hasn't been seen for several weeks. "Not to worry," the porter says, "those blokes walk around with their heads in a cloud." I fear that he's too close to the mark.

I call Cal's friend and editor, Frank Bidart, who hasn't heard from him either. We both worry that Cal has had a relapse of the mania that has been kept well in check thanks to the new drug, lithium.

Finally a cryptic telegram arrives. PERSONAL DIFFICULTIES MAKE TRIP NEW YORK IMPOSSIBLE RIGHT AWAY. LOVE, CAL

At my urging, Frank flies to London.

LONDON

Frank waits to tell me what he discovers until he is back in New York and we can meet in person. Cal is living in London with a new woman. Actually not new to any of us, as she used to be the girlfriend of Ben Silvers, the editor of the *New York Review of Books*, and in that capacity has been to dinner several times at our home. I remember seating her next to Cal. She was clearly intimidated and when she finally ventured a remark about the soup being delicious, Cal, who was quite drunk, barked that it was hideous, and she froze. He apologized and kissed her hand, something I'd never seen him do before. Was it her title? Or her beauty?

Lady Caroline Blackwood, an heiress to the Guinness legacy, is rail-thin with midnight hair and eyes and translucent Irish skin. She is a talented writer and fifteen years younger than Cal and me. Her first husband was the painter Lucian Freud, grandson of Sigmund. She is separated from her second husband, Israel Citkowitz, the celebrated successor to Aaron Copland, and the father of her three daughters. Although there are rumors that Ben Silvers is the sire of her youngest.

Caroline was at the Faber and Faber party, Frank tells me, and Cal, claiming it was too late to go back to Oxford, asked to spend the night at her London townhouse. And never left. "He's in love with her," Frank says, with a sigh. "Only to be expected," I say. "Cal is always falling in love and it always presages a manic episode." "So what do we do?" Frank asks. "Wait for the hospital's phone call?"

No, I think. Not this time. I remember what Cal's father told me on my wedding day, that now I would be responsible for him. Could it be time to transfer that responsibility? Caroline has the money and the connections to take care of him. I imagine a life without Cal. The freedom of it. The stability. Being able to plan and follow through, thinking only of Harriet and me. Cal has always taken up too much space in any room he enters, pushing everyone else against the walls. What would it be like to be able to have a room of one's own?

The call comes a week later. Cal is hospitalized at a private clinic outside of London. His psychiatrist inquires about his lithium dosage. Apparently Cal has not taken his medication in several weeks and is having a full-blown attack. "Where is Caroline?" I ask. The doctor is reticent at first, but when I persist he tells me that Lady Blackwood's mental health is fragile. She suffers from clinical depression and has decided it's best that she and her daughters remain in her Irish estate.

She has abandoned Cal when he is most in need. "What kind of love is it," I ask the doctor, "when you can't be sick?"

Frank and I fly to London, drive to the clinic. Cal is weak and disoriented. He is heavily tranquilized and can only manage to stay awake for a few hours. He's lost weight. His hair is shaggy. His clothes are dirty and disheveled. We take him to a barber shop, buy him new clothes. He asks for some books . . . Dante, Shakespeare and Chaucer.

In a few days, he regains some strength and regales his fellow inmates with readings of choice passages. He is recovering. Caroline gives strict instructions to the doctor to forbid Cal's returning home with me. Not that he's voiced the desire.

The day before Frank and I are to leave, she shows up in the hospital. Cal is delighted to see her, envelops her in an enormous bear hug, then covers her face with kisses. I need to turn away. He clearly is besotted. And so is she.

When Cal is released she will put him up in a studio near her London manor house, and when he is fully recovered he can move back in with her. Until then, she says it will be hard on her children not to see him. And what of my child?

LETTERS

Cal is back living with Caroline. He writes in his studio but returns to her in the evenings. He needs to be with a family, needs a woman in his bed. He writes to me almost daily now. Poetry is pouring out of him. Personal poetry. Confessional poetry. He is writing about his dilemma. Harriet and I are the dilemma. He is deeply in love with Caroline. But he does not want to lose us. He is a creature of habit, firmly engrained in the rituals we have developed over our twenty-year marriage. He cannot imagine his life without Harriet, without being a guide and witness to her change and growth into womanhood. So he must leave Caroline. But how?

I take heart. It is just another fling. An aftermath of another manic episode. Just get a plane ticket, I write. I'll take care of the rest. As I always have. I recall the angry letters containing unpaid bills once sent to him by a fiery flamenco dancer he seduced and ensconced in a fine hotel. Distraught, he paced our bedroom, flinging her letters onto the rug. I picked them up and paid the bills. He was grateful, filled with remorse. "Build a fence, Lizzie," he implored, "Brand me like a steer."

But then he writes that he will stay in London for the summer. That this is not the usual manic romance. That although he fell in love with Caroline when he was sick, he is now well and still in love with her.

I am furious. You have caused great harm, I write. I have had to break the contract about subletting our apartment and studios at a significant financial loss. I have given up my teaching appointment at Barnard, and they have replaced me for the year. I have withdrawn Harriet from Dalton and they have no more openings. Your selfishness as you pursue your pleasure is unconscionable. My utter contempt for both of you for the misery you have brought to two people who have never hurt you knows no bounds.

Cal writes back immediately, begging me to forgive him. He is not in his right mind. He cannot survive without me.

I feel, to a large extent, that is true. He has come to depend on my rationality, my common sense, my willpower, my ability to bring peace and order to our lives. I contain him. And yet there is a part of him that wants to go wild, a raging river that wants to overspill its banks like the Nile, flooding the plains, so that new crops can grow. The fertile delta. Cal finds that in erotic love. And this time he has not found it in a schoolgirl or an infatuated groupie. He has found it in a grown woman, beautiful and gifted, and as careless and crazy as he is.

The letters continue over the weeks and months. In one letter he will return. In the next he will stay in England. Each letter is as impassioned as the one before and the one after. Each makes arguments for why that choice is the only possible one.

On Harriet's birthday, a particularly heartfelt missive. Will I take him back? Will I forgive him? How can he make it up to me and Harriet? Has he destroyed our family forever? Has he lost the one thing in life that he values most?

These pleas alternate with declarations as to why he must abandon us. He needs to be in love to write. Our marriage has been without eros for so long it cannot be revived. England is a more compatible place for him to live. Harriet and I are better off without him. People change and move on.

I remind him that he is a consummate American poet. His roots are in the historic soil of New England. I implore him to honor his legacy, his talent, his native voice and return to the country of his origin.

He is moved and sees the truth in my painting of the bigger picture. He lives for his work. He understands America, its idiom, its complexities and contradictions.

And then in the next letter he declares he must break

free of old and limiting ties. Create himself anew. Otherwise he will suffocate and die.

This vacillation continues for seven months until I can no longer bear it. I ask Frank to write to him on my behalf. To tell Cal in no uncertain terms that he is wrecking my health and turning Harriet into a neurotic, insecure adolescent at a time when she needs stability most. Frank tells Cal he must choose.

And so he does. I get a letter. His love for Caroline has been proven. He has never been happier or more creative in his life. It has lasted the test of time. A full year. He wants to marry her.

A full year. What is that against our two decades? Marry her? That part is new. Always in the past, once the mania lifts, he has been relieved to return to me and to Harriet. To where he belongs. In the sanctuary of the home we've built together, whether in Boston or New York, surrounded by his parents' vintage furniture that we've inherited, the good paintings and books and records we've collected. His bathrobe hanging next to mine, his toothbrush leaning on mine, his slippers in the closet, stepping on the toes of mine.

I sit with the letter in my lap, pour myself a decisive glass of bourbon. This cannot go on. I think of Beckett's *Endgame* . . . "I can't go on. I will go on." Is that the condition of life? God gives us what we most need and then takes it away. What a bargain!

A NEW LIFE

Cal writes to tell me that Caroline is pregnant with his child and they are both "over the moon." Cal is fifty-five, Caroline forty. She is big as a house, he says, and they are both exhausted and spend their days lying on the couch. He remembers my being much more energetic when I was pregnant with Harriet, but this is Caroline's fourth bout and, he supposes, it takes its toll. They are both drinking and smoking less and compensating for the deprivation by over-eating. The three little girls are thrilled about the new baby, and he hopes Harriet will be as well. Would I please give her the good news?

I hate being his messenger and acquiesce only because I know it will be less traumatic if I tell Harriet in person. I insist that he follow up with a letter, which he does. It is a tearful business for both Harriet and me.

We don't hear from him for a while. He has not been well, he explains, suffering from serious nosebleeds due to his high blood pressure. Or perhaps it's a sympathetic response to Caroline's condition?

And then I get a cable. Eight pounds, bright red, a veritable gingerbread boy. Mother and son doing well. Robert Sheridan Lowell is in the world.

So he's given the baby his name. Marriage cannot be far off.

He writes to Harriet. "You have a baby brother. We're calling him Sheridan, after Carolyn's ancestor, the renowned Irish playwright, Richard Brinsley Sheridan. His best known play is *The School for Scandal*. Perhaps you've read it?

"I can't wait for you to meet your new brother. You may even take delight in having a brother so much younger than yourself he is almost of another generation. Talking British and having my face or something of me, of you.

"I want you to know, darling Harriet, that there can never be a second you in my heart.

"Dear Heart, give all my love to mother and to yourself . . . alas we can never give it all, I try. Love, Daddy"

DIVORCE

After the birth of Sheridan, I file for divorce. I've heard that despite her two previous marriages, Caroline, in the style of wayward aristocrats, has no desire for another marriage. She feels it deadens spontaneity. It is Cal, the New England puritan, who wants the sanctity of the church, of officialdom.

He shall have his divorce and I will make him pay for it. Pay for all the pain and humiliation his actions have caused. I get a lawyer who works out a generous settlement for me that includes the Manhattan apartment, together with all tangible personal properties—furnishings, works of art, household goods, and the interest on Cal's trust fund. Cal calls it a barracuda settlement. A bone of contention is the Castine, Maine house that his cousin Harriet Winslow has left to me. Cal argues that he should have half ownership as it's his relative. I refuse, saying that she left it to me precisely because she didn't trust him to take care of it.

"She knew you too well," I tell him. "You're a careless man, Cal. You lose things. In your wake, you shed shirt buttons, manuscripts, money. Your cigarettes burn holes in the sheets."

We negotiate the further details of our estate on trans-Atlantic phone calls. Some of our talks are combative, heart-wrenching. Others are neighborly. He admonishes me for spending all my alimony on these frequent and lengthy calls. "What's money for?" I answer, and he congratulates me on my newfound attitude.

Perhaps if I had been less practical, I might still have him. But that way lies misery. He is gone. Living in a new country with a new wife and a new family.

POST-DIVORCE

Cal and I are now formally divorced. After all the months of tortuous vacillation, the actual process, as Cal describes it, seems faintly ludicrous. He and Caroline fly down to the Dominican Republic and, in a grass hut with chickens underfoot, Carolyn divorces Israel Citkowitz and Cal divorces me. Then with their papers in hand they pad over to an adjacent hut, take their marriage vows, and fly back to London.

I ponder relinquishing my married name and then decide to keep it. I've always written under my maiden name, Elizabeth Hardwick, and will continue to do so. But Elizabeth Lowell will make Harriet's life smoother, and I am still the point person for Cal's archives. Indeed, he still addresses letters to me as Mrs. Robert Lowell.

Harvard has matched Stony Brook's offer, and I am spending hours every day in sorting and filing. Cal is an incessant reviser. For every poem, and there are thousands of them, he has multiple versions. If not for Frank Bidart tearing them out of his hand, they would never get to the publisher.

Cal's multiple, half-finished, conflicting versions cause chaos. In his work, in his life. He doesn't want to choose. He wants them all. And when it gets to be too much of a mess, someone will sort things out for him. Someone like me. But I am running out of strength.

I need to retrieve myself. Preserve myself. I will never be entirely free of him, nor do I want to be. We have shared twenty momentous years and the fate and future of a young beautiful soul, our daughter. Despite my fury with Cal, I manage to conceal most of it from Harriet. She loves and needs us both. Cal and I correspond frequently to discuss Harriet, and when he invites her to visit him and Caroline, I acquiesce. They are now living in Kent at one of Caroline's ancestral estates, with majestic grounds and lots of domestic animals. She will love being there, Cal exults, and is grateful for my kindness in allowing the visit.

I am apprehensive for her safety, though, as she is only fourteen. I require Cal's numerous assurances that he will meet her at the airport, closely supervise her entire stay, and see that she gets on her return flight. Cal is famously forgetful, and I've heard tales about the disorder in their household. Caroline hires indifferent staff, fires them, and finds even worse replacements. Dust balls roll through their drafty house, ashtrays overflow, food rots on forgotten plates, empty wine bottles are strewn across the carpet. I'm told that Caroline doesn't even bother to kick them under the sofa, the sign of an unrepentant aristocrat.

But none of this bothers Harriet. Not having a sibling, she is entranced with the Blackwood girls and the *laissez-faire* attitude in the household. And to her delight, she spends several days in London alone with Cal. She tells me he has a new fascination . . . dolphins.

For a farewell present, he gifts her with an antique pin studded with tiny diamond chips in the shape of an arrow. He tells her that it points directly to his heart.

DOLPHINS: THE ANIMALS

Cal writes that he is indeed obsessed with dolphins and has bought a year's membership to London's recently opened Dolphinarium on Oxford Street. He visits daily to watch Bonnie and Clyde, the two resident dolphins, perform. At the signal of their trainer, they leap out of the water and offer their flippers for a handshake. They retrieve a cowboy hat and a bonnet thrown into their tank and swim back to their trainer wearing them. The Dolphinarium also hosts two seals, two penguins and six Aquamaid showgirls in bikinis. Cal assures me that he's only interested in the dolphins.

They are amazing creatures, he states, mammals that mate belly to belly like humans. Indeed, the male dolphin at the Dolpharium has to be treated with anti-androgens to keep him from making sexual advances to the Aquamaids.

Cal inundates me with his research. The name dolphin comes from the Greek *delphus* (womb). Hence, they are fish with a womb.

The male is called a bull, the female a cow, the babies calves. They lack a sense of smell, but have an eye on either side of the head giving them two fields of vision compared to our binocular view.

They are one of the most intelligent animals on Earth, their brain-body ratio second only to humans. They travel in large pods and have a complex language of clicks and whistles, which they use both to communicate and for echolocation.

Cal fills pages with their exploits and special abilities. They can teach, learn, cooperate, play, scheme and grieve. They are compassionate and will stay with ill or injured members of their pod and even bring them up to the surface to breathe.

He is so enamored that he buys all manner of dolphin-themed objects, including four antique and pricey stone statues to place on either side of both the drawing room fireplace and the front door. Caroline objects to their size and expense, he writes, but the little girls love them and dress them up like dolls.

I am puzzled by Cal's sudden passion for marine life and then I find out why. It's the miraculous rescue.

THE RESCUE OF ARION

Arion, a legendary poet and musician, is said to have invented the dithyramb, the choral poem performed at the festival of Dionysius. None of his works survive and only one story about his life is known, reported by the historian Herodutus.

After a successful performing tour of Sicily and Magna Graecia, Arion sails for home. The sight of the treasure he carries arouses the cupidity of the sailors, who resolve to kill him and steal his wealth. He is given the choice of suicide, after which his body would be buried on land and receive the proper death rituals, or being flung overboard, where his body would be lost at sea and his spirit doomed to wander forever and never find rest.

Arion begs permission to sing a final song accompanied by his lyre. He then throws himself overboard and is miraculously saved by a dolphin who is charmed by his song. He lives a long and prosperous life, and when he dies his lyre and dolphin are placed among the stars, becoming the constellations Lyra and Delphinus.

RUMORS: THE *DOLPHIN* POEMS

I hear rumors that Cal is writing a major new collection of poems. A sort of novel in verse. Autobiographical, current, confessional. When he calls, I question him about it. He says it's still a work in progress, although, he has already sent Elizabeth Bishop a draft, as he usually does.

"Does she like it?" I ask.

"She calls it 'an act of infinite mischief.' "

"What's it about?" I ask.

"The events of the last year."

"Our marriage?" I ask.

"Among other things."

"Our divorce?"

There's a long pause and then a quick demurral: "Don't worry about it, Lizzie. You come out very well. The protagonist, some people think. Shall I send you a copy?" Another long pause, this time on my side.

We've been divorced for a year now. I am putting my life back together, and it's actually better than the sixty percent I envisioned. I think it's seventy-five percent. I'm much in demand as a reviewer, and for short opinion pieces in well-paying magazines like *Vogue*. And I get to write long critical essays for the *New York Review of Books*. If I compile them, they might make a book—essays about the wives, sisters, and daughters of famous literary men and how those women surrendered their own time and talent to further the careers of their men. I'd call it *Seduction and Betrayal*.

So many helpmeets to choose from: Sylvia Plath, Zelda Fitzgerald, Dorothy Wordsworth, the Brontës. And then there are the fictional ones: Ibsen's Nora, Hardy's Tess of the D'Urbervilles.

"Lizzie?" Cal says. "Are you still there?"

"I'm here."

"I thought I lost you."

"No, just thinking. Never mind sending me a copy. You'll revise it so much that by the time it's published it won't be recognizable," I say.

"Are you sure?"

"Absolutely."

I am to regret that hasty certainty, although at the time it seems to be in my own self-interest. My own self-protection. I'm writing fluently and well. No matter how it's expressed, the material in Cal's new book will upset me. His work is confessional. Even if he doesn't name names, anyone in the literary world will know about

Divine Madness

whom he's talking. As for myself, I have always been discreet.

No doubt I am working through some of my own personal issues in my essays on betrayed women, but they are veiled. In examining the lives of literary women, I am not divulging the particulars of my own heartbreak and fury. I am not *washing dirty linen* in public, a dreadful cliché I'd never use in an essay, but this is a private document *for my eyes only*. Oh, Lord, another cliché.

This domestic outpouring invites it. I need to steer away from it in my book, widen the scope beyond melodrama, couch it in history, economics, politics. Even Cal sees the mediocrity of *the same old story, one man and two women*.

I am feeling increasingly strong and independent. Cal has the right to record the events of his life in any way that he chooses. How can it hurt me?

THE DOLPHIN: PUBLICATION

The first notice I get about the publication of *The Dolphin* is a review in *The Nation* by Marjorie Perloff, from the University of Maryland:

"It is Lizzie who becomes the dominant figure in the sonnets, and she is depicted, perhaps unwittingly, on Lowell's part, as Dark Lady or Super-Bitch par excellence. Poor Harriet emerges from these passages as one of the most unpleasant child figures in history . . . her cloying moral virtue. It is therefore difficult to participate in the poet's vacillation, for Lizzie and Harriet seem to get no more than they deserve."

I am devastated. I vowed not to read Cal's book until I finished writing *Seduction and Betrayal*, but I rush out to the nearest bookstore. I feel ridiculously conspicuous, as if I should be wearing a disguise. But the clerk hands me a copy with an innocuous smile. "I'm sure you'll enjoy it. We've been selling it a lot. I hear it's pretty juicy for a poetry book."

Harriet is at a friend's house for a sleepover so I have time to read the book cover to cover. By the time I'm finished, I am sobbing and the rescue bottle of bourbon is at half mast. How dare he hold us up to such public scrutiny! *The Dolphin* maps out the last three years of strife. Cal's falling in love with Caroline, his vacillation about leaving us, my tormented letters veering from pleas for him to return to recriminations and threats. The difficult divorce. The immediate marriage to Caroline. The birth of Sheridan. His newfound happiness and productivity with his dolphin, his mermaid, his Circe.

All of it is scalding, humiliating, but the unforgivable part is the cruelty towards Harriet, the exposing of her vulnerability. Displaying her private loss and sorrow to public criticism and ridicule.

I call him immediately, disregarding the time difference. I can tell by his bearish grumble that I've woken him. Good! I hope he never sleeps again! I read him Perloff's review. He brushes it off. "She's a nonentity just trying to make a name for herself by being nasty. Ignore it."

"I cannot ignore it," I shout. "You've humiliated me and you've done irreparable harm to Harriet. I never want to speak to you again." I slam down the phone and drink myself to sleep.

The Dophin does not fare well with our friends. Although their critiques, I fear, are more loyalty towards me than an appraisal of the quality of the poetry. Still I am grateful for them.

And for the letters they had sent trying to dissuade him from publishing.

TWO LETTERS

From the Poet Laureate, Stanley Kunitz:

"As for *Dolphin*, I should be less than honest if I didn't tell you that it both fascinates and repels me. There are details that seem to me monstrously heartless. I will grant that parts of it are marvelous—wild, erotic, shattering. (Who else had the nerve for such a document of enchantment and folly?) But some passages I can scarcely bear to read—they are too ugly, for being too cruel, too intimately cruel. You must know that after its hour has passed, even tenderness can cut the heart.

"What else need I say to you, dear Cal, not as your judge—God save me!—but as your friend."

From the poet Elizabeth Bishop:

"It's hell to write this, so first do believe that I think *Dolphin* is magnificent poetry. It is also honest poetry—almost. I feel I must tell you what I think. I love you so much I can't bear to have you publish something that I regret and that you might live to regret, too.

"There is a mixture of fact and fiction and you have changed Lizzie's letters. That is 'infinite mischief' I think.

"The letters, as you have used them, present fearful problems: what's true, what isn't; how one can bear to witness such suffering and yet not know how much of it one needn't suffer with, how much has been 'made up.'

"One can use one's life as material—one does anyway—but these letters—aren't you violating a trust? IF you had been given permission? IF you hadn't changed them? But art just isn't worth that much."

Cal's response :

"Let me rephrase for myself your moral objections. It's the revelation, with documents, of a wife not wanting her husband to leave her, and who does leave her. That's the trouble, not the mixture of truth and fiction. Actually my versions of her letters are true enough, only softer and drastically cut. The original is heartbreaking, but interminable."

A POET'S REVIEW OF *THE DOLPHIN*

Adrienne Rich on *The Dolphin* in *American Poetry Review*:

"There is a kind of aggrandized and merciless masculinity at work in this book.

"What does one say about a poet, who, having left his wife and daughter for another marriage, goes on to appropriate his ex-wife's letters written under the stress and pain of desertion, into a book of poems addressed to the new wife? If this question has nothing to do with art, we have come far from the best of the tradition Lowell would like to vindicate—or perhaps it cannot be vindicated.

"At the end of *The Dolphin*, Lowell writes:

I have sat and listened to too many
Words of the collaborating muse
And plotted perhaps too freely with my life,
Not avoiding injury to others,
Not avoiding injury to myself—

Lynne Kaufman

To ask compassion . . . this book, half fiction
An eelnet made by man for the eel fighting—
My eyes have seen what my hand did.

"I have to say I think this is bullshit eloquence, a poor excuse for a cruel and shallow book, that it is presumptuous to balance injury done to others with injuries done to one's self—and the question remains—to what purpose? The inclusion of the letter poems stands as one of the most vindictive and mean-spirited acts in the history of poetry."

Cal responds by stating that the woman's movement has turned Adrienne into a zealot and a man-hater. There is some truth to it. I, too, take issue with ardent feminism when it turns all men into the enemy. My world would be poorer without men even though many of their acts are reprehensible.

A SAD POSTSCRIPT

After Adrienne Rich left her husband and three sons for a lesbian relationship, her husband walked into the woods and killed himself.

MY DEALINGS WITH THE PUBLISHER OF *THE DOLPHIN*

I write to Robert Giroux, the president of Farrar, Straus and Giroux, who I had thought was a good friend.

How could you have published this without asking my permission for the prodigal use of my letters, I exhort.

I have since been analyzed in print, given some good marks as a wife and mother, and in others disparaged and rebuked. I and my young daughter have been exploited in a supposedly creative act under our own names and in our own lifetimes.

And since the facts are not truly facts because of their disguise as poetry they cannot be answered.

I had not seen these poems before, and I felt it was undignified of me to insist, but the reality of them is disturbing far beyond anything I could imagine.

There are so many wrong impressions—nothing about my acceptance of the separation, my willingness to divorce, the return of the good spirits and contentment of myself and my daughter.

I wish to go on record as to how saddened and deeply resentful I am of the use of my letters without permission and the many ill-effects it has had upon me. I have never been so hurt in my life.

MY LETTER TO ELIZABETH BISHOP

Thank you so much for your kind letter. I feel truly awful about Cal's book, hurt and sad. And even worse, the parts about me and Harriet are so inane, empty, unnecessary. I cannot understand how three years of work could have left so many bad lines there on the page. That breaks my heart for all of us.

A CONVERSATION WITH CAL ABOUT *THE DOLPHIN*

CAL

Most people see you as the heroine of *The Dolphin*. The wronged one. The noble one.

LIZZIE

You had no right to use my letters.

CAL

They were sent to me. They were mine.

LIZZIE

I could have sued you. I talked to a lawyer. In the matter of correspondence, the actual letter and envelope belong to the recipient, but the content belongs to the writer.

CAL

I didn't use them verbatim.

LIZZIE

That's the point, Cal. In my letter I wrote, "I don't entirely wish you well." In your poem quoting my letter you wrote,

"I don't wish you entirely well."

CAL

Same exact words.

LIZZIE

But a different order. A different meaning. Your words mean I don't wish you entirely healed. That's much more damning than, "I don't entirely wish you well."

CAL

Which means?

LIZZIE

That I have some conflict, some withholding of my good wishes for your general happiness.

CAL

You're parsing words, Lizzie.

LIZZIE

We live by words. Here's another. In my letter to Caroline about Harriet's upcoming visit to London. I wrote, "Harriet knows that she will have very little of him from now on, and that he belongs to you and all your children since his physical presence there and absence here is the most real thing." And this is how you transcribed it, "She knows she will seldom see him; the physical presence or absence is the thing."

Divine Madness

CAL

I shortened it.

LIZZIE

You turned my prose into lead. Flattened the pain and loss. Don't tell me you don't see the difference.

CAL

Poetic license. I paraphrased it. Made it my own.

LIZZIE

Those were my words, Cal. You needed to ask permission.

CAL

Would you have given it?

LIZZIE

Of course not.

PRIZE

Robert T.S. Lowell, Emerson Lecturer in English Literature at Harvard University, wins the 1974 Pulitzer Prize for Poetry for his book of verse *The Dolphin*. The honor makes Lowell the only poet besides Robert Frost to garner the Pulitzer Prize twice. The $1,000 prize is given by the trustees of Columbia University upon the recommendation of an advisory board of unnamed jurors.

Poetry Jury Report for 1974 (Secretary's Note)
Professor William Alfred of Harvard, Chairman of the Poetry Jury, and Professor Anthony Hecht of the University of Rochester both selected Robert Lowell's *The Dolphin* as their first choice for the Pulitzer Prize in Poetry. The third juror, Gwendolyn Brooks, felt *The Dolphin* was "unworthy" and appended a report recommending three black poets. She was overruled by the other two judges.

THE NEXT THREE YEARS

Cal's friend, Jonathan Raban, sends me an article he's written about Cal's working method of constantly revising.

"For Robert Lowell revisions are a kind of gaming with words; he treats them like billiard balls. His favorite method of revision is simply to introduce a negative into a line which absolutely reverses its meaning but very often improves it.

"For example, in his poem about Flaubert dying, in the first draft he writes, 'Till the mania for phrases dried his heart.'

"Then he sees another possibility and writes 'Till the mania for phrases enlarged his heart.'

"It makes perfectly good sense either way round, 'enlarged' or 'dried,' but they happen to mean the opposite of each other."

When I read this, I have an "aha" moment. That's Cal, all right, walking between the opposites. He sees the truth in both sides. That's why he's so infuriating. And so captivating. And has so much trouble knowing his own mind. Unlike me.

Although I admit, when in the midst of emotional turmoil, I may veer towards extremes, as I do when I tell Cal I never want to speak to him again. But when my fury abates, I know I will always maintain contact. That he is irreplaceable and incurable.

SEDUCTION AND BETRAYAL

I was once asked if I had felt overpowered by Cal's work, meaning did it overpower my own. "Well, I should hope so," I said, "I have great regard and admiration for it."

Not the remark of a proud feminist. But the truth of it is that in a marriage of two creative people, one person's work and needs take priority. Even in my enlightened set, we women were expected, and expected ourselves, to put ours as secondary.

So with the rewards and burdens of Cal's presence removed, I am able to get a prodigious amount of my own writing done.

I publish *Seduction and Betrayal: Women and Literature*, my collected essays from the *New York Review of Books*, in which I consider the lives of literary women.

Dorothy Wordsworth, William's sister . . . "She lived his life to the full."

Zelda Fitzgerald, Scott's wife . . . "Her passionate wish for self-reliance and personal freedom was dismissed as self-deception."

Jane Welsh, wife of Thomas Carlyle . . . "Her married life began as very much a union with Mrs. Carlyle cleaning, dusting, chasing bedbugs, sewing, supervising redecorations, ever conscious that for all her wit, she was playing a great role in the creation of Carlyle."

The union faltered when Mr. Carlyle began to spend too much time with Lady Ashburton, thus breaking the unspoken contract of a wife and her works.

In the long run wives are to be paid in a peculiar coin—consideration of their feelings. And it usually turns out this is an enormous inflation few men will remit, or if they will, only with a sense of being overcharged.

SPERM SISTERS

It's a colorful 60s coinage for women who've shared lovers. During my "salad days," when I was sleeping around, we didn't call it anything. We eschewed the labels "promiscuous" or "slutty." We were liberated. Except for my one abortion, which was somewhat traumatic as it was illegal, there were no negative consequences.

I rarely suffered from jealousy or regret when the flings ended. It was just sex. With Cal it was and still is different.

It is three years since I last saw him. We write and phone often, sharing news about our daughter, our writing, mutual friends. Our exchanges are cordial. We are on our best behavior. Now comes an invitation. Harriet is planning to visit Cal and Caroline over spring break. Won't I come, too ? The invitation is proffered by both of them and reinforced by Harriet. If things are really okay, she asks, why not make the visit? Pretty please?

I spend the evening visualizing the encounter, rehearsing various scenarios. I won't stay with them, that's for certain. I can't possibly be witness to them heading up the stairs to their shared bed while I wave gamely from the sofa. No, if I go, I'll treat myself to a luxurious hotel and make my visit as brief as possible.

I pour myself a stiff bourbon, close my eyes and summon an image of Caroline when I last saw her, when she was an amusing curiosity at my dinner table. She was Bob Silver's girlfriend then. Not a danger, no more so than any other young and exotic creature. The world is filled with beautiful women willing to be dazzled by America's leading poet. It's the combination of his ursine earthiness and his refined esthetic that allures them. They long to enter the musky circle of his strong, furry arms and be transformed. He nibbles on their tender flesh until he is no longer amused and then he ends it. They are teary-eyed but leave, with a juicy story to tell at literary cocktail parties.

Every muse but Caroline. Caroline is now wife to Cal and mother of his child. A dual honor only I had held. Ay there's the rub. I pour myself another bourbon, take a big slug, and feel the pleasant woolliness arise.

What do I miss the most? Not sex. Our sex life the last few years of our marriage was perfunctory. Cal had trouble getting it up. Although we cuddled in bed and held hands, and I miss that. I still have the apartment and the house in Maine, and our circle of friends and books, and records, and theatre, and my writing, and my darling Harriet, and Sumner the cat.

Divine Madness

What I miss most is married life. Having a partner. Having a family. Shared meals. Shared talk. Shared money. Shared space. And having Cal read his new poems to me. That I am the first person to hear those thoughts. To feel his eyes fixed on my face, hungrily awaiting my approval.

I miss Cal needing me, in good times and bad. Caroline cannot handle his mania. It exacerbates her alcoholism and depression. She needs to leave Cal when he gets ill.

"But what kind of love is it, when one can't be sick?" I asked Cal's London psychiatrist that question and he didn't answer.

I'll answer it now. That's not love. That's not family. Robert Frost got it right . . . "Home is the place, where when you have to go there, they have to take you in."

VISITING CAROLINE AND FAMILY

Cal offers to meet me at the airport but I prefer taking a taxi. I am determined to be as independent as possible. When I ring the doorbell of the London mansion, I am tempted to turn tail and run. But I stand my ground, knees weak, chest pounding. Luckily it is Harriet who answers the door and flings her arms around me. She laces her fingers through mine and leads me up three flights of stairs, knocks on a closed door. "This is Caroline and Daddy's flat," she explains. "The children live in another wing. That's where I stay."

From inside, Caroline's refined English accent wafts. "Come in. Come in. Door's unlocked."

I enter a large, lavishly furnished drawing room. Cal and Caroline are lying on adjacent divans. They struggle to their feet, obviously sloshed. Cal shakily kisses my forehead as Caroline waves a greeting. "Wine or gin and T?" she asks.

I opt for gin, and we engage in some small talk as Harriet drifts away. "You're looking very well, Lizzie," Cal offers. And I return the compliment. They do look well, both of them. I have conveniently forgotten what a beauty Caroline is, those enormous eyes, prominent cheekbones, the bone-thin model's body. She wears a clinging black silk shift, her only ornaments an armful of gold bracelets and heavy black mascara. She is distinctive, memorable. Next to her, I feel very much Lexington, Kentucky.

The dinner she serves helps to even the score. It consists of fillets of a bland white fish drowned in an equally tasteless white sauce. The silverware is tarnished, the glasses are spotted, and the tablecloth stained. Fortunately the wine is excellent and plentiful. It's just the three of us at the table. The children dine with their nannies.

Caroline tells me how much she enjoyed *Seduction and Betrayal*. I congratulate her on her book reviews for the *Times Literary Supplement*. "You've got to read her latest," Cal says and hands me a copy of Caroline's review of Nancy Friday's best seller, *My Secret Garden*. The book is a compilation of women's sexual fantasies that Caroline finds repetitive and dull. She reads an excerpt:

"A woman, Bertha, who dreams of being bound and raped by a donkey while three black men are watching doesn't seem significantly different from a woman, Betty, who dreams of being bound and raped by three black men while a donkey is watching. Instead why not use what's readily available, such as a vacuum cleaner, a battery operated toothbrush, or a shower nozzle." Then she adds with a sly smile, "And there's always the family poodle."

I laugh out loud.

Encouraged by my response, she relates a ribald story, a true one. Some years ago, pre-Robert, she returned to her townhouse in Greenwich Village, after renting it out, to find a rack, stocks and a crucifix in the basement. There were whips and chains in all the corners and every object in the house seemed to have a sinister purpose. In addition, the phone kept ringing with callers voicing extreme and bizarre requests. To amuse herself, Caroline pretended to be the madam and quoted highly inflated prices for acts of bondage and discipline. No one ever quibbled, she said. And the children called it "Mummy's brothel."

Clearly I have underestimated Caroline. She and I spend the rest of the evening sharing anecdotes while Cal, feeling left out, retires for bed early. He tells me later how deeply relieved he was at how well the two of us got along. I think he would preferred to have us fighting over him.

Instead I told Caroline about the time he absently put a lit cigarette in his pajama pocket and set himself on fire. In return she asked if his nose-picking habit bothered me?

ROBERT SHERIDAN LOWELL

Cal is delighted with his baby son. He writes about him frequently in his letters.

He describes Sheridan, bright red after delivery, as a bartender who imbibes or a lobster-colored gingerbread man.

A few months later, he chronicles Sheridan chewing on everything in sight including his blanket, his parents' fingers and the little dog.

As Sheridan becomes more mobile, Cal writes that he is already a University of Virginia type, untidy, boisterous, good fraternity material. He has also destroyed books, short-circuited a third of the house, and pushed over a section of the fireplace.

I remember Cal being fascinated by Harriet as she morphed from infant to toddler. Not that he ever got involved in the day-to-day care. It was more like the visits of a busy grandparent, although he made time for trips to the zoo, museums and boat rides.

I'm not the sort of parent, Cal writes, who plays catch in the back yard, but Sheridan seems to like me well enough. Probably because I don't toss him up in the air and call him "manly."

From friends, I hear that Sheridan looks uncannily like Cal. And that he is a child who is never once said no to.

CAROLINE'S RAGE

When Caroline's father died, her brother inherited the family home, Clandeboye, and the title. What should have come to her as the firstborn did not, merely because she was a woman. She felt a deep rage about things that women weren't allowed to do or be. Despite having married three prominent artists, she was not content to be a muse nor coast on her beauty. She wanted to be known for her own accomplishments.

Unfortunately she did inherit the Guinness gene for alcoholism and when she was drunk she became difficult.

I start hearing rumors that their marriage is in trouble. Although, at first, Cal praised his new and idyllic life with a dolphin who "spouts the smarting waters of joy in your face . . . who cuts your nets and chains," after seven years with Caroline, he is beginning to see her as one of the destroying Sirens.

MORE ABOUT
CAROLINE BLACKWOOD

Caroline's mother, Maureen, the Marchioness of Dufferin and Ava, was a flamboyant socialite. Her son called her villa in Sardinia "Villa Costalota." Her idea of fun was to turn up at houses of society hostesses wearing a comedy penis nose with a fart machine hidden between her legs. Once she was so drunk, she fell over and smashed the family tiara.

Caroline's parents lived in London while she and her brother grew up in an ancestral stone mansion called Clandeboye in County Down, Northern Ireland. Her great-grandfather built not merely a room, but a wing every time another child was born. The place was terribly run down, with pails to catch dripping water all over the place.

Caroline carried garlic in her handbag. Chefs stinted on it, she said, and she liked to chew on the cloves.

CAL AS ULYSSES

Writers live in metaphor. We talk about character arc and a protagonist's journey. Joseph Campbell reintroduced us to the monomyth, the universal story of the hero's adventure.

We are all heroes of our life's adventure. For Cal, he was Odysseus.

> Speak memory of the cunning hero,
> the wanderer, blown off course time and again.

> Sing to me of the man, Muse
> The man of twists and turns

These are separate translations from the Greek of the opening lines of the *Odyssey*. When it comes to describing Cal, I need both. Is it the tsunami of his manic depression that repeatedly blows him off course or is it his own desire for twists and turns? And are they not inseparable?

I would not call Cal cunning as he is not calculated. More instinctual. Impulsive. He acts first and then finds a rationale for it. I've read that the new findings in neuroscience back that up for all of us. A throwback to our primitive reflexes. That rustle in the bush could be a snake. We dart out of its path before we discover it's only a wind-swept branch. False alarm. But if it were a snake, we would have avoided its bite. Cal is closer to his primal instincts. The lizard brain.

And the metaphoric brain as well. But then, so am I. It's a matter of training and practice. A search for meaning. A desire to connect our everyday emotions and events with something larger, more lasting. A bid for immortality.

The *Odyssey*, an epic poem, is the oldest extant piece of Western literature, a survivor of the burning of the Great Library of Alexandria. It is a tale of Odysseus— warrior, trickster, serial adulterer—and his ten-year journey to return from the Trojan War to his home in Ithaca and his loyal and faithful wife, Penelope.

Along the way he becomes a lover and prisoner of the nymph Calypso on her sweet-scented isle, a lover and prisoner of the enchantress Circe who turns men to swine. As his ship sails past the Sirens, he orders his sailors to plug their ears with wax to protect them from the Sirens' songs luring them into the sea to drown. But he himself must hear them, and he commands his men to tie him to the mast. And no matter how he pleads, they are not to release him. They don't, and he finds his way home without further incident. Would that were our personal fate.

"And so, Penelope, too, rejoiced, her gaze upon her husband.

"Her white arms around him. Pressed as though forever."

So for Penelope it is a tale of undying loyalty. For decades, ten years of the Trojan War and ten years of Odysseus's adventures, she has been courted by suitors eager to marry her. She has put them off by declaring that she must first finish weaving a burial shroud for Odysseus' father. She weaves the shroud every day and unravels it each night.

Finally, she declares that she is ready to choose her next husband. Each man must attempt to string the massive bow of Odysseus and plunge an arrow through the handles of twelve war axes.

Odysseus, disguised as an old beggar, is the only man who succeeds. Penelope tests him further by commanding him to bring her marital bed into the courtyard. He replies that he cannot, for the marital bed is built around an oak tree.

Penelope recognizes him, and Athena restores the wizened beggar to his young and virile self. He disposes of all the suitors and carries off Penelope to their bed.

The return of the prodigal husband. Is that to be my future? Well, none of the other women, goddesses though they are, can keep him from returning home.

Lynne Kaufman

I think about the symbolism of the warp and the woof, the vertical threads constant as the sun, the horizontal threads temporal as the moon. The opposites that join in the final tapestry: the male and female, the seeking and the knowing. I think about T.S. Eliot. "We shall not cease from exploration and the end of all our exploring will be to arrive where we started and know the place for the first time."

AN INTERVIEW WITH THE *PARIS REVIEW*

I teach creative writing at Barnard College.

This is what I tell my students.

I do not believe creative writing can be taught. The only way to learn how to write is to read. A passion for reading can be shared. Nevertheless, I offer my axioms:

There are only two reasons to write: desperation or revenge.

You can't be a writer if you can't take rejection, which is why sometimes after reading a student's story, I say, "I'd rather shoot myself than read that again."

How I work:

Sometimes, like Virginia Woolf, I'll read poetry to find my way in, to open my mind.

Where I work:

I type at a desk upstairs in my apartment on West 67th Street.

I type on a heavy machine on my dining room table.

I write in big handwriting on legal pads that then wait on tables for my doubts.

I write in little notebooks that I tuck between the cushions of my red velvet sofa.

I write with books piled all around me, open or face down, that ask me questions or whisper about the way in.

Reading
The greatest gift is a passion for reading. It's cheap, it consoles, it distracts, it excites, it gives you knowledge of the world and experience of a wide kind. It is moral illumination.

Thinking
One day I visit Mary McCarthy and Hannah Arendt is there, lying on the sofa with her arms behind her head, staring at the ceiling. "What's she doing?" I ask Mary. "She's thinking," Mary says, "composing in her head."

I am in envy. I don't know what I think until I write it down, and my first drafts look as if they've been written by a chicken. It's only when I'm revising that I know why I've chosen this life. For me, writing is almost a physical process, and I never understand why I can do it on a Wednesday and not on a Friday. But I sit there until I find a way in, until I get it right, until it's finished. I am cursed with perfectionism. It is not genius; it is self-sabotage.

Divine Madness

Robert Lowell's Influence
Cal has a great influence on every aspect of my life. His immense learning and love of literature are a constant magic for me. The poet's prose is one of my passions. I like the off-hand flashes, the quickness, the deftness, the confidence and the relief from spelling everything out plank by plank.

The Problem with Writing
No matter what you write, story, essay, novel, once you are finished, you have to do it all over again, have to start on something new. Writing is not a collaboration. In the solitude of the blank page, everyone is up against their own limits.

Danger
To express yourself is to expose yourself, to seize the stage is to risk humiliation. You must develop the moral courage to trust your own experience in the world and your own intuitions on how it works.

Inspiration/Perspiration
Charles Lamb, the nineteenth-century essayist, perhaps best known for his treatise on roast pig, was appalled when he gazed upon the drafts of Milton's "Lycidas" in the library of Trinity College, Cambridge and saw that the poem had not been delivered to the poet complete, by the

angel Gabriel, but haphazardly through second and third thoughts.

"How it staggered me to see the fine things in their ore! Interlined, corrected! As if their words were mortal, alterable, displaceable at pleasure! As if they might have been otherwise, and just as good! I will never go into the workshop of any great artist again. I wish the librarian had thrown the draft pages into the Cam River."

For another opinion: Samuel Beckett
"Ever tried. Ever failed. No matter. Try again. Fail again. Fail better."

ON BIOGRAPHY AND HERMAN MELVILLE

"Call me Ishmael." The consummate first line. The iconic American novel. Although I have said that biography is a scrofulous cottage industry done mostly by academics who get grants and have a good time going all over the place to interview, if asked, I would write a biography of Melville.

Mine would be a featherweight against the doorstop Melville biographies that precede it. My work is fragmentary. Human beings are ultimately unknowable.

"Melville is elusive, the facts of his life only a frame. This often unhappy man knew many happy days: or was it that this more or less settled gentleman had periods of desolation? All is true, if you like."

ABOUT HERMAN MELVILLE

Melville's parents came from prominent families, yet they had endless financial problems. The Melvilles seemed to have a genetic disposition to bankruptcy. His father died when Herman was thirteen, leaving the family penniless.

Melville was thirty-two when he wrote *Moby Dick*, his fifth book. He had a wife and a child, another child on the way, and dubious prospects of ever supporting his family through writing.

The book was tantalizingly subversive, if not affirming at least forgiving of the blind destructiveness of human nature and nature itself.

This self-described "thought-diver" into the truth of the human heart turned bitter when the public failed to embrace *Moby Dick*.

The same year in which he wrote *Moby Dick*, he fell in love with his Berkshires neighbor, Nathaniel Hawthorne, and was rejected by him. This disappointment, which coincided with the critical and commercial failure of his novel, left Melville heartsick and in a social and philosophical retreat for the rest of his life.

He developed a cool, backhanded acceptance of his destiny, a pride in failure, which he capitalized as a kind of deity.
　　Although his masterfully wrought work was rediscovered in the 1920s, he died in poverty and obscurity.

Melville's long-suffering wife, Elizabeth Shaw, the daughter of an illustrious Massachusetts judge, stayed married to Melville for forty-four years. She endured her gifted husband's frustrations, long silences, drunkenness, withdrawals and possible violent rages.

Is it any wonder that I relate more to Elizabeth Shaw than to Melville? Mary always said that I buried my autobiography in my critical texts.

This from my essay on Ibsen's *Rosmersholm*:
　　"Heaven is not likely to send a desperate, strong-willed woman of thirty an interesting unmarried man. No, it will send her someone's husband and tell her to dispose of the wife as best she can."
　　Prescient? Or simply, as the youngsters say, "What goes around comes around."

SLEEPLESS NIGHTS: A NOVEL

It is said that all writing is autobiographical. I would add that memoir is the least truthful. Even if I could be objective, I am not interested in revealing my secrets. *The Dolphin* did more than enough of that. So *Sleepless Nights* is mostly about ideas and other people. It is a work of memory and invention, not driven by narrative but by what Henry James called "the life of the mind."

It is a novel without a plot, with a protagonist who shares my name and follows the known contours of my life but allows itself to shift its attention from one person or situation as abruptly as a filmmaker. It uses the resources of the essay, journal, memoir, and poem. It chronicles life with the blanks left in and all the questions that flourish in those blanks. Unanswered, unanswerable questions, finding resolution not in a full stop but in a question mark.

THE RESIDENTS OF THE HOTEL SCHUYLER

In my twenties, I lived at the Schuyler Hotel on 45th Street in New York City. It was cheap and in the heart of everything I wanted to be part of. The residents were not poverty-stricken, just always a little "behind." They were not spinsters but divorcees, not bachelors but seedy *bon vivants*—deserters from family life, alimony, child support, from loans long erased from memory. They drank three days and sobered for three.

Most of them were failures, but they lived elated by unreal hopes, ill-considered plans. There were many performers at the Hotel Schuyler but they gave no hint of suffering from failure. Rather than calling it art, they called it employment.

Old age was unimaginable. Perhaps lovers would turn into widowers in the nick of time, somebody somewhere would settle a little property on them. How the Schuyler

Hotel night clerks envied the tenants . . . the lucky ones we never pass by in life without asking: What do they live on?

MY ROOMMATE J

At the Hotel Schuyler I lived with a red-cheeked homosexual young man from Kentucky in a *mariage blanc*. We were as obsessive and jealous and cruel as any ordinary couple. His corrosive neatness inflamed me at times. In the evening he carefully selected and laid out his clothes for the next day, for his job which he despised. Worst of all, he had an unyielding need to brush his perfect teeth after dinner . . . no matter what.

J died when a car went out of control at a crossing and struck him as he was patiently waiting for the light to change.

BILLIE HOLIDAY

J introduced me to jazz and to Harlem.

I revere Billie Holiday as perhaps the most fully realized individual I've ever met. I write: "Never was any woman less a wife or mother; not even a daughter. I love her violent perfume and her splendid head, archaic, as if washed up from the Aegean."

Her work took on, gradually, a destructive cast, as it so often does with the greatly gifted who are doomed to repeat endlessly their own heights of inspiration.

A brilliant performer done in by racism.

I abhor the attitudes towards black people that dominated my Southern upbringing. So many injustices suffered by Negroes. We continue to write about them . . . Selma, Alabama; the Watts Riots; Martin Luther

King's assassination. But little is done. How hard it is to keep the attention of the American people.

YOUNG COUPLES

"Beginnings are always delightful, linger on the threshold," Goethe said.

There are streets in the Nineties where affluent young couples buy townhouses, taking off the stoop so that drunks can't loiter, making a whole floor for the children to be quiet on, then divorcing because the strain and the cost of building drive them to separate. The neighborhood is called Death Row. People say, "Strange, they were much happier than we were."

ON DIVORCE

It is easier for any man, young or old, rich or poor, to turn a few corners and bump into marriage.

Two women recently divorced ask me: "Are you lonely?"
    "Not always," I say.
    "That's marvelous," the first one says, smiling.
    The second one adds gravely, "Terrific."

I am alone here in New York, no longer a "we."
    No longer do I speak of "ours," that tea bag of a word which steeps in the conditional.

MY FATHER

When he was in his coffin, my father was very handsome, his hair parted on the wrong side, his profile reminded everyone of John Barrymore. He was not well educated but intelligent, read a great many true detective stories and newspapers. He sang beautifully and knew the words to many, many songs. He worked as a laborer and as little as possible.

He was political and so was I. We got up early to listen to the radio during the fall of Madrid. We held hands and wept.

In Maine when men come to fix things, I think of my father and flirt a bit. I like their sunburned faces, their finely oiled work shoes, jokes about the bill, their way at the wheel of a truck. I wonder what it would be like to be married to a man like that. To see him coming out of the shower, to have dinner at six, lights out at nine, frequent lovemaking in honor of the long day of working, up at five, visit the relatives on Sunday.

MY MOTHER

My affectionate, tireless mother had eleven children. Her femaleness was absolute and ancient. When the subject of childbearing was raised, she would shrug and look perplexed. Or sometimes she would say, "It did not make me miserable, if that's what you want to know."

THE OLD BARN

I have sold the big house in Maine and will make a new place to live, beginning with the old barn. I mourn the sloughed-off house.

I remember Harriet Winslow, Cal's favorite aunt, and her worn recording of Gluck's *Orfeo ed Euridice*. I hear the music and see her very tall, old, with her maidenly beauty. The smell of the leaves outside dripping rain, the bowls of nasturtiums , the orange Moroccan cloth hanging over the mantel. I will never cease to love the old lady who gave the old house and barn to me . . . alone.

ONLY PASSAGES ABOUT CAL IN *SLEEPLESS NIGHTS*

"How is the Mister this morning? Josette K would say. The Mister? Shall I turn his devastated brown hair to red, which few have? Appalling disarray of trouser and jacket and feet stuffed into stretched socks. Kindly smile, showing short teeth like his mother's."

LETTER FROM MARY MCCARTHY ABOUT *SLEEPLESS NIGHTS*

I wonder what Cal would think. He'd be put out somewhat in his vanity to find himself figuring mainly as an absence and an absence that the reader doesn't miss.

I like your idea of wondering whether you might not change his hair color to red--- very funny, and it demonstrates how little his "thisness" matters rather than his mere "thatness." He becomes a black hole to be filled in ad lib, which is poetic justice. He's condemned, by the form you've chosen, to non-existence. You couldn't do that in a conventional autobiography. Brava!

LETTER TO MARY MCCARTHY ABOUT *SLEEPLESS NIGHTS*

Oh, Mary, when I think of the people I have buried, North and South. Yet, why is it that we cannot keep the note of irony, the jangle of carelessness at a distance? Sentences in which I have tried for a lighter tone and many of those have to do with events, upheavals, destructions that cause me to weep.

CRITIQUES OF *SLEEPLESS NIGHTS*

You may discard all the "givens" of the realistic novel—but you will still require something to bind the shreds of disassociated consciousness into a whole. Miss Hardwick has staked too much on the idea itself, and forfeited much in the telling. It is a work of "negative capability."
— Diane Johnson

Negative capability is when a work is capable of being in uncertainties, mysteries, doubts without any irritable reaching after fact and reason.
— John Keats

If I want a plot I'll watch *Dallas*.
— Elizabeth Hardwick

FAMILIES OF CHOICE

I am the ninth of eleven children. My older siblings were far more of an influence on me than my parents. I feel gratitude for their benign neglect when I think about Cal's claustrophobic childhood. The nuclear American family is a petri dish for neurosis, declared Margaret Mead from her enviable vantage point in Samoa.

Since my parents' opinion of me mattered very little, I could become whom I wanted, not by rebellion but by desire. My family of choice was the *Partisan Review*, the men I worked and slept with, the women whom I befriended and with whom I competed.

Foremost among them is Mary McCarthy. She is well ensconced in the *Partisan Review* circle when I first meet her. It's at a cocktail party at the Rahvs'. Most Saturday nights there is a cocktail party attended by the writers and editors and their wives. A crowded, smoke-filled living room, everyone already drunk on Four Roses bourbon, shamelessly flirting, shouting in intellectual discourse.

Mary is the prettiest woman in the room and the most elegantly dressed. Her shiny black hair is caught in a tight bun emphasizing her classic profile and large brown eyes. She is holding court, surrounded by attentive men. She may write like a man, which is a high compliment at *PR*, but at a party she's very much a woman. I admire that about Mary, how she prides herself on her domestic arts, especially her cooking. She declares that the obligation to serve a first course at a dinner party ought to be written into the Bill of Rights.

It turns out that we've both been lovers of Phillip Rahv. Indeed Mary has lived with Phillip for several years before, one night, she drunkenly sleeps with the literary critic Edmund Wilson and marries him. It's a mystery why she leaves Rahv, her Levantine lover as she calls him, with his thick unruly hair and wrestler's build, for Wilson, a plump ungainly fellow with a face like an overripe squash. That marriage, her second of four, lasts seven years, and includes being beaten by Wilson when she is pregnant with her only child Reul and being institutionalized by Wilson, against her will, for hysteria.

Mary believes in candor on the page and in life. She spares no one the details of her amorous exploits, beginning with the loss of her virginity at the age of fourteen. Perhaps it is the recital of those erotic escapades that edges Wilson

Divine Madness

to violence. And some say she gives as good as she gets. She certainly is the more fit and agile of the two.

I admire Mary. We are alike in both being prolific and ambitious writers, but she is much more visible, notable, quotable. Mary seems so confident, so sure of her opinions and judgments. Instead of openly competing with her, I surreptitiously hope to be her closest friend.

Unfortunately that position is already filled by someone far more illustrious . . . Hannah Arendt, a European intellectual, a fugitive from Nazi Germany, who also writes for *PR* and writes brilliantly. Hannah is the real thing . . . an original thinker, a true philosopher. The author of *Eichmann in Jerusalem*. The creator of the phrase "the banality of evil," which rains censure on her head from every observant Jew, not to mention her alleged love affair with Martin Heidegger.

Mary thinks that Hannah and Cal are the only actual geniuses we know. The rest of the crowd are merely clever. And I agree.

Hannah often invites Mary and me for drinks in her Riverside Drive apartment. Her husband, Heinrich Blücher, greets us and disappears into his study. Although his love affairs are well known in the *PR* circle, he is discreet, and since we all know that Hannah is his intellectual superior, it balances the score. Just as Cal's mania balanced my steadfast acceptance.

Hannah serves us cocktails as well as cake and coffee, which we find a delightful European eccentricity.

Our conversations range widely, but no matter the subject I can feel the heightened attention that Mary gives to Hannah's utterances on matters of the mind (ideas, history, politics) and that Hannah gives to Mary's observations on matters of daily life (dress, decorate, dining).

Some people don't realize when they're superfluous, but I am sensitive to it. I feel it in the air when people are drawn to each other. A charged vector of electricity. The way they lean forward, aligning themselves with the posture of the person they're attracted to. The mirroring of gestures, the intensity of eye contact. The chosen pair listen to each other with laughter, sighs, clucks of agreement. They say, "Tell me more," and when one raises a new topic, the other listens avidly and expounds on it.

And I feel like the outsider, the third wheel (there it is again, any time I move towards trying to express emotions, I come up with these humiliating clichés). Is there no time when a third wheel can be useful . . . say on a shopping cart? What about a three-legged stool? A tripod? Or a triangle? Wasn't it Oscar Wilde who quipped that the chains of matrimony are so heavy it takes two to bear them

Divine Madness

. . . and sometimes three. It turns out, when I look it up, to be Alexander Dumas. But it still sounds like Oscar Wilde. My mind is wandering as I try to recreate those conversations, just as it did when they were actually happening, when I was pondering why I wasn't equal in their eyes to each other. But then again . . . how do you make someone love you?

THE GROUP

Maybe that's why I write that parody of *The Group* in *PR*, and even though I sign it with a nom de plume, Xavier Prynne, it is clear to everyone in our circle who wrote it.

Mary McCarthy's novel about eight young privileged women at Vassar has topped the *New York Times Best* bestseller list for two years and brought her popular recognition and, more importantly, lots of money. Somehow Mary has figured out ways for her writing to support her in great style. And, despite the sneers of the literary establishment, *The Group* becomes required reading for young women throughout the country. Although set in the 1930s, almost thirty years earlier than its publication, it provides a detailed and frank description of sex, contraception and breastfeeding. It causes such a scandal that it is banned in Australia.

Norman Mailer, a man whose own writing does not shy away from graphic depictions of sex, dismisses it in the *New York Review of Books* as "a trivial lady writer's novel infused with a common odor that is a cross between Ma Griffe and contraceptive jelly."

So I am surprised at how outraged Mary is by my mild satire. I call my article "The Gang," and it begins like this:

"Maisie had always, rather demurely, thought of the great event as 'defloration,' from the Late Latin, *defloratio*. (To everyone's surprise, this sociology major had been a whiz in Latin at St. Tim's). She was deflowered on a floral divan. Mother would, somehow, have minded the odious couch more than the 'event.'"

I only write as Xavier Prynne one more time, and my target is Norman Mailer:

"All the Bitch did was blow into my ear—one of those mysterious pre-psychotic Jackie Kennedy whispers. My answer to the FBI would run this way: The existential orgasm would make atomic war and even atomic testing impossible."

It's too easy, making fun of other writers. We each have our own particular and recognizable habits of style. Is it laziness or a mark of individuality? When I think of my own convoluted sentences, I prefer the latter. Be yourself, as the wag advises, everyone else is taken.

At any rate, the literary trouncing of *The Group* is nothing like the enmity aroused by Hannah Arendt's *Eichmann in Jerusalem*, which is published that same year.

THE BANALITY OF EVIL

When Hannah Arendt learns that Adolph Eichmann, the executor of "the final solution," has been captured in Buenos Aires by the Mossad and is to be tried in Israel, she implores William Shawn, the editor of the *New Yorker,* to send her to Jerusalem to cover the trial. "It is an expensive request as the trial is expected to last for almost a year," she says, "but I feel it is an obligation I owe to my past."

To her surprise he agrees. Under Shawn, the *New Yorker* is shedding its reputation as a lightweight publication by commissioning serious journalism like James Baldwin's *The Fire Next Time*, John Hersey's *Hiroshima*, and Rachel Carson's *Silent Spring*. Hannah's reporting is printed in five issues of the *New Yorker* and shortly after published as a book.

BAD REVIEWS

One of the most important duties of literary friendships is to assuage the hurt feelings that a bad review brings. And no matter how many favorable reviews a book gets, it is the bad ones that you remember. Indeed, the most damning phrases become memorized, for they have unearthed the very inadequacies you hope to conceal. That's when you need a friend to tell you the reviewer is jealous, mean spirited and vindictive. Forget about it. Move on.

It is Mary who comforts her through the critical onslaught. I am *persona non grata* as Hannah thinks I'm the one who lined up Lionel Abel to write the damning review of her book in *PR.* It is actually Phillip Rahv who wants to bring her down a peg, and knows that Abel has already published extremely negative reviews of Hannah's previous work.

Hannah anticipates that her book will cause controversy, but doesn't expect that she will be labeled "a self-hating Jew," or that the Anti-Defamation League of B'nai B'rith will call for her excommunication and for rabbis to denounce her from the pulpit during the Jewish high holy days.

Although Hannah defends her book as attempting not to be a treatise about the Holocaust but simply to present a journalistic report about one trial, two of her findings cause outrage. One is her modifying Eichmann's evil with the word "banal,'" and the other is revealing the complicity of European Jewish leaders.

The first objection comes from the misunderstanding of the use of "the banality of evil." Arendt is not undermining the import of the genocide. She is not calling the Holocaust banal. The banality refers to Adolph Eichmann, who instead of being a raving, fanatical monster is, in actuality, a bumbling traveling salesman for the Vacuum Oil Company of Austria. So how can such an ordinary man, an ill-informed, inarticulate, ideologically apathetic, unimaginative bureaucrat, bring himself to participate in the slaughter of millions? This shrunken, gray-faced creature on trial, "the man in the glass booth," claims he was just following orders. He is found guilty, hanged, cremated and his ashes thrown into the sea. Arendt doesn't judge him, society does.

Her second point is even more incendiary. She documents how Jewish leaders helped in their own people's destruction. She writes about how Jewish police rounded up their fellow Jews and handed them over to the Nazis. She documents how Jewish councils prepared lists of Jews that the Nazis used in emptying out the ghetto.

She postulates that if the Jewish people had really been unorganized and leaderless, there would have been chaos and suffering, but the total number of victims would have been much less. To a Jewish audience, the role of the Jewish leaders in the destruction of their own people is undoubtedly the darkest chapter of the whole unbearable story.

Arendt writes of the submissiveness of the Jews, how they would walk to the places of execution, dig their own graves, make neat piles of their clothing, and lie down to be shot. But she also writes of what happens when the victims dare to resist, how the Nazis slowly torture four hundred Dutch Jews to death in revenge for one single act of defiance. She acknowledges the impossible moral choices.

But perhaps it is also her tone, the dispassionate language of reason and argument, that draws such ire, that causes her to be charged with a failure of sympathy, a lack of soul.

I wonder if a male author dealing with those atrocities would be critiqued so harshly or instead be praised for his cool and disinterested eye.

There is another factor which Mary and I, as gentiles, speculate about. It seems to us that the American Jews, whom we know, bear a reservoir of guilt about not being more active in helping European Jewry. Hannah taps into the long-suppressed rage and grief evoked by the Holocaust.

American Jews prefer turning their attention to the new state of Israel, to the birth of Zionism in the hope that something good might come from all that horror. In fact, American Jewish intellectuals fight Hannah more zealously than they fought Hitler.

Norman Podhoretz writes in *Commentary*:
"In the place of the monstrous Nazi, Arendt gives us the 'banal' Nazi; in the place of the Jew as virtuous martyr, she gives us the Jew as accomplice in evil, and in the place of confrontation of guilt and innocence, she gives us a collaboration of criminal and victim."

Lionel Abel in *PR* accuses Hannah of making Eichmann aesthetically palatable and his victims aesthetically repulsive.

The uproar over the book continues to rage in the intellectual press for almost three years. It dies down briefly around the time of the Kennedy assassination, only to flare up again afterward. Mary says the "Eichmann Business" is taking on the proportions of a pogrom.

HANNAH'S STORY ABOUT EICHMANN

Eichmann was never troubled by anything he had done to the Jews, in general. But he was bothered by one little incident; he had slapped the face of the then president of the Jewish community in Vienna during an interrogation. God knows many worse things were happening to people than to be slapped in the face. But he never condoned himself for having done this. He had lost his cool.

HANNAH ARENDT AND MARTIN HEIDEGGER

He is her philosophy professor at the University of Marberg. She is seventeen. He is twice her age, married to Elfriede and the father of two boys. He is writing his masterwork, *Being and Time*; she is writing her dissertation on Saint Augustine and Love. She is his most gifted student, a Jewish beauty with raven hair and classic features. They fall in love. It lasts for three years, clandestine, passionate, literary. Hitler rises to power. Hannah flees to Paris, marries a fellow refugee, and emigrates to the United States.

Meanwhile, Heidegger joins the National Socialist Party and becomes the rector of the University of Freiburg. He defends his choice on purely intellectual grounds, that he has no political interests, but he accedes to the expulsion of all Jewish students and professors in the University.

Hannah keeps in touch with Heidegger for the rest of her life. She uses her influence to get his books published in the States. For her, his character flaws pale beside the brilliance of his mind and his role as her mentor teaching her how to think.

When she visits him in Germany, she agrees at his request to call his wife Elfriede, a virulent anti-Semite, by the familiar "du."

Hannah must dismiss Heidegger's reprehensible behavior in order to maintain her unbending devotion to him. For her, he is the king who reigns in the realm of thinking. For both, passionate thinking and aliveness are one.

Is that how I deal with Cal?

HANNAH DIES

Hannah Arendt is in the midst of a dinner party at her New York apartment, lighting yet another forbidden cigarette, when she dies of a heart attack. It is five days after she has finished writing the second volume of her projected trilogy *The Life of the Mind*. *Volume One: Thinking* and *Volume Two: Willing* remain to be edited. *Volume Three: Judging* is a single page in her typewriter.

Mary McCarthy abandons her own half-finished novel to spend two years editing Hannah's manuscript. What greater gift to a dead friend? But Mary needs a live friend, too. And that becomes me.

MARY'S AWARD

Mary is to be awarded a prestigious medal and asks me to introduce her. I have introduced Mary many times before. We're seen as a natural match. Age, gender, the *Partisan Review*.

Mary gives an elegant and idiosyncratic speech.

"In accepting the award, I've been driven to review my career, a somewhat saddening business, for I, as a person and a writer, seem to have had little effect, in the sense of improving the world I came into or even maintaining a previous standard. The only improvement I can see is in the proliferation of labor saving devices, which I see as no progress at all.

"Michelangelo spoke of leaving some mark of the tools on the marble rather than having a smooth polished surface. I think that has something to do with the truth.

"I like labor intensive implements and practices. The amount of labor that goes into a human manufacture determines the success of the enterprise."

I can vouch for that. Mary likes cranking an ice cream freezer by hand. Pushing a fruit or vegetable through a sieve. She fights off the electric typewriter and the Cuisinart. She refuses to get a credit card, claiming she is against the forced registration of citizens, and therefore has to carry awkward amounts of cash.

"Why should I care that I have lived my life as a person and a writer in vain? We all live our lives more or less in vain. We should not hope to count for something. As writers we can hope to give pleasure to some and as a bribe that will persuade them to listen to us when no pleasure is involved."

That's Mary talking about her political journalism and mine. We come from a time when serious writers felt an obligation to make their opinions about social injustices, clandestine wars, uncontrollable greed known. We believed that writing was important. In truth, we felt that writing was everything.

Through no fault of our own, people like Mary and me are becoming marginal. We are seeing the death of intellectual life in America. The culture has moved away from words and ideas to images. And those of us who have fought for an enlightened welfare state, social democracy and racial equality are old and tired.

Divine Madness

And yet, this story brings me cheer.

Kurt Vonnegut and Joseph Heller are at a party hosted by a billionaire in his Long Island mansion, with his uniformed staff, string of polo ponies, stable of antique cars. Vonnegut says to Heller:

"Our host makes as much money in one day as you've made in a year on *Catch-22*."

"But I have something he'll never have," says Heller.

"And what's that?" Vonnegut demands.

"Enough," says Heller.

MARY ON THE UNRELIABILITY OF MEMORY

Although Mary's utmost virtue is truth telling, she reflects on the way that memory fuses events and details, perpetuating misunderstanding. A favorite story is about her son Ruel, who at the age of six was waiting with Mary for the local bus. When it came, the driver leaned out the window with the latest piece of news. "They've thrown Mussolini out," he shouted.

Mary says it took years to convince Reul that the Italian dictator had not met his end by being thrown off a bus in Cape Cod.

SEVENTH YEAR

Cal's marriage to Caroline is indeed foundering. The causes are myriad and manifold. The similarities that brought them together now loom as insurmountable obstacles. Cal cannot write in the turmoil and drama of Caroline's household among the boisterous children, the inept staff and the decaying mansion. Caroline, terrified by onsets of Cal's mania, retreats into alcohol and depression. They cannot live together. Each needs a caretaker. They make each other worse. They are more than two explosions. They are two earthquakes.

Cal has just finished teaching the spring session at Harvard. Carolyn and the children have remained in Ireland, where she has moved for tax purposes. Cal visits me in New York. He is pale, his frame shrunken and stooped. He believes he doesn't have long to live. Both his parents died at sixty, the age he is now. He has just been diagnosed with heart disease. He is distraught, in a quandary. He wants to move back to the States, but not give up Caroline and the children. He has suggested to Caroline that he make periodic long visits to Ireland, that he be a frequent visitor. Caroline, of course, will have none of it. Caroline does not believe in sharing. Nor do I. Not anymore. Although from the look of things, Cal is not up for much. He is spent.

I tell him I am leaving for Castine next week. He asks to join me. Maine is a healing place for him. I have sold the old house and am living in the remodeled barn, I tell him. There is no place for him. He'll rent a studio, he says, and promises not to intrude on my life. There are many mutual friends summering there, and Mary McCarthy will be hosting parties for the New York literary set. How can I say no? I don't govern the town of Castine. And Cal finds a nice little boathouse on the beach.

SUMMER IN CASTINE

One night, several weeks in, I invite Cal to dinner. He brings a bottle of champagne and eats every morsel of food that I've prepared. He uses the last biscuit to mop up the gravy. "I've missed your cooking," he says. "I think you've missed any kind of cooking," I counter. "Sardines and soda crackers," he admits. "I've stockpiled them."

So I invite him again. And it soon turns into a pleasurable evening routine. We work separately during the day, then Cal heads up to the barn for a few drinks, dinner, listening to favorite records, and Cal goes back to his boathouse. Of course our crowd notices, and there's some gossip, or what we writers like to call character analysis.

I confide in Mary McCarthy. Explaining the situation to her helps me clarify it for myself. "There is no great renewed romance, but a kind of friendship. Mostly I listen to his grief about Caroline. He's learned something from being 'unwanted' by Caroline. It's made him more like the rest of us. If he believed Caroline would really want him, I think he would return immediately. But she wouldn't for more than a week.

"I am not nearly as vulnerable to Cal as I used to be, but I still care for him.

"I don't feel as if I'm undergoing an approval process, nor do I care about contracts and commitments. We are just going along, having a very agreeable time." I pause, trying to sum up my feelings. "I guess, at the age of sixty, we are trying to work out a sort of survival for both of us."

LABOR DAY

My time at Castine traditionally ends after the Labor Day weekend. By then I'm eager to get back to the clamor and bustle of Manhattan. To theatre and films, book readings and restaurants. To serious work, deadlines and competition. To real life.

I help Cal pack up his few belongings in preparation for his return abroad.

"Will you be living in England or Ireland?"

"Neither, "he replies, "I've had my fill of being an expat, I'll be teaching at Harvard."

"That's a surprise."

"A good one?" He flashes a meta-message smile that I ignore.

"So you'll be living in Cambridge?"

"Commuting from New York," he says.

"You have a place?"

"Sixty-seventh Street. It's a great neighborhood."

"Always was."

He pauses, "And a great apartment." He waits, letting the silence build.

"Not a good idea, Cal."

"Why not?"

"That train has left the station."

He casts me a look of mock disapproval. "Not like you to use a cliché, Lizzie."

"Not like you to become one."

Cal flinches and I am immediately remorseful. I can be sharp and vituperative. This is not a fair fight. "I'm sorry."

"So am I, Lizzie. I never meant to hurt you or Harriet. I love you both. With all my heart."

He stares at his shoes. "Why is it when we speak our deepest truth it comes out in platitudes?"

"It's the difference between feeling and thought," I venture.

"Neurologists say that emotion comes first and then we try to describe it."

"Yes, I've read that." We are in the more comfortable realm of abstraction now. Cal's color returns to normal. My hands stop shaking.

"We can both use a drink," Cal says and pours us each a stiff one.

With drinks in hand, we retire to the porch, take adjoining rocking chairs and gaze out at the ocean.

Cal downs his drink and waits for me to finish mine.

I sip, stalling for time, until he takes it from me. He rises slowly, painfully, and stands behind me, his hands on my shoulders.

I know what to expect, and I brace for it.

"Let me come home, Lizzie." His voice is imploring, but I can resist that. It's his touch, the way his fingers curl around my shoulders that moves me. The fit. The comfort. Like slipping under the covers on a wintry night. His hands linger on my shoulders.

During our month in Castine, we have not touched other than a glancing brush of fingers in passing. Was that deliberate? If so, on whose part? And why have I denied myself the pleasure of this communion? I have been so lonely.

How am I going to tell Harriet?

HARRIET

"You're not going to let him move back in," she says, her tone more command than question.

"For a little while."

"Bullshit. Don't you remember how awful it was when he left?"

"Of course I do."

"Then why open yourself to that abuse again? You're doing so much better without him."

"In some ways."

"In every way. Don't give in."

"He says this time it's for good."

"And you believe him!"

Do I? I hesitate, unsure. And then it no longer matters. An answer bursts forth, from such a deep part of myself that it seems to be spoken by someone else. "This is his house and everything I have, including you, is his . . . everything. He is worthy of care."

"You are hopeless." Harriet slams down the phone.

I start to dial her number to explain. But how can I when I don't understand it myself? Seven years have passed. Seven years of healing, of becoming myself, of being Elizabeth Hardwick and not Mrs. Robert Lowell.

It took hundreds of letters and phone calls to end the marriage. Years to dissolve the emotional bonds, parcel out the financial holdings, the shared belongings, the mutual friends. And now in one question and one reply we are to return, to mend, to become whole again. How is that to happen?

And that moment was the starting point of this reflection. This memoir. Will Cal return to me? Do I want him to? And under what conditions?

PHONE CALL

Three days before he is to return to the States, I get a phone call from Dublin. Will I accept the charges?

It is Cal. "The visit was torture. Caroline and I fought all the time. She wants me back, but we're no good together. She's left for London with the children. I've got a flight to JFK arriving at six in the evening."

"Shall I meet you at the airport."

"No, I'll take a cab. See you at the apartment."

I call Harriet to tell her, not knowing what to expect. Happily, her mood has lifted. I invite her to join us for dinner that night, but she is marching in a demonstration with other Columbia University students to protest the killing of the apartheid hero Steven Bilko.

"Come by later," I urge. "Dad will be interested in hearing about it." Cal has told her of his political activism: refusing to serve in the Korean War, marching against the war in Vietnam, boycotting LBJ's invitations to the White House.

"It'll be too late," she says. Then, just before she hangs up. "Give him my love."

THE TAXI

The elevator man rings on the intercom. A taxi has arrived. Can I come down? Cal is asleep and unresponsive in the back. On his lap is a large parcel wrapped in brown paper. I get in beside him, and we drive the eight blocks south to Roosevelt Hospital, where he is pronounced dead. On the death certificate I list Caroline Blackwood as surviving spouse and identify myself as Elizabeth Lowell, a friend.

The doctor hands me the parcel and I bring it back to the apartment. I unwrap it carefully, as if the paper holds a message that will explain what has just happened. It is a portrait of Caroline painted by her ex-husband, Lucian Freud, called "Girl in Bed." It shows a young Caroline, leaning forward on her elbow, her eyes enormous. My heart clenches. He brought her with him. He could not be without her.

Where was he going to hang it? In the foyer? In the living room? Over our bed? And where would I have allowed it? In his study where it would be secreted, viewed only by him? Or would that have been worse? I stare at the painting as it rests upon my knees. It is a semblance, a replica of Caroline. Paint on canvas, not flesh on bone. Painted in a hotel in Paris when Caroline was twenty-two, Cal once told me. It hung in Caroline's London dining room. It was worth a lot of money and considered one of Lucien's finest works.

I place the painting on a high shelf in a back closet, face down. I chastise myself for being jealous. Doesn't Cal carry pictures of me and Harriet in his wallet and briefcase? I am speaking of him as if he's alive.

I looked at his body a long time in the hospital room, memorizing his features, the length and strength of him. His face in repose seemed mildly surprised. I touched his hand, his fingers still warm against my cold palm.

I wanted to kiss him, but as I knelt, my knees were so stiff, I lurched forward. The doctor saved me from a fall and I was too shaken to try again. He guided me to the door and I did not protest. An attendant put me in a taxi. It was all done in a kindly and efficient manner. Death, to them, is an everyday occurrence.

I must call Harriet. She will be comforted that her final words to her father, though undelivered, were "give him my love." Would that "love" was always our parting word . . . for some day it will be our last.

ARRANGEMENTS

I am the one to call Caroline and tell her the news. At first she is contained and formal, but when she hears that Cal died alone, she breaks into hysterical sobs. She and the children will fly to New York immediately. Can they stay with me?

And they do so for a full week. A week during which I get no more than two hours of sleep a night. Caroline stays awake, drinking heavily, speaking incessantly, sometimes incoherently. There are two questions I long to ask, but cannot summon the courage. Did he say he was coming back to her? And what about the painting?

Robert Giroux, Cal's publisher, informs the press, and the ensuing obituaries are laudatory and voluminous. For me, the most trenchant is: "Robert Lowell died, in a New York taxicab, as he left the ashes of his third marriage for the embers of his second."

With the help of Cal's lifelong friends, Peter Taylor and Blair Clark, and his editor Frank Bidart, I arrange for the funeral service. It is a solemn Episcopalian requiem mass held in the Church of the Advent on Beacon Hill in Boston, near where Cal was born and spent his childhood. More than six hundred mourners attend. They come from the quiet tree-lined neighborhood around the church, from New York, from Europe.

From the high pulpit, Peter Taylor reads "Where the Rainbow Ends," the last verse of *Lord Weary's Castle*. "I saw the sky descending, black and white, Not blue on Boston, where the winter wore the skulls to jack-o'-lanterns on the slates."

The Reverend Collingwood adds, "Robert Lowell knew intimately and painfully those dark chaotic forces forever threatening the firmament."

Caroline and I catch each other's eye as we nod in agreement. She wears no make-up other than heavy mascara, which is now running in black rivulets down her cheeks. Surveying the many notables in the group . . . Richard Wilbur, Saul Bellow, William Styron, Derek Walcott, Susan Sontag, Norman Mailer . . . she murmurs, "You could take it on tour."

As the encomiums to Cal flow, Mary McCarthy tempers them with a whispered, "The biggest whitewash in history."

Elizabeth Bishop is quietly weeping. I think of the poem Cal wrote for her. "We wished our two souls might return like gulls to the rock. In the end, the water was too cold for us." He was in love with her, asked her to marry him. She refused, although she opined later that she would have liked to have a child with him.

A Chekhovian missed moment. The thing that almost . . . but doesn't happen. That instant of being on the verge of taking an action that will change your life. But you don't. You play it safe.

Later, you regret it, try to retrace your steps, but the crossroad is gone.

In my life, I took the leap and "that has made all the difference."

REVELATION

I am standing with Caroline and her children as they wait for the taxi to take them to the airport and back to London, when I finally ask the question. Amidst the traffic noise, I need to repeat it.

"The painting 'Girl in Bed' that Cal was carrying . . . "

"Oh, yes," she says. "Do you have it?"

I nod.

"He was bringing it to New York for me to have it appraised. Tax purposes."

"I can do that . . . if you like."

"That would be brilliant. Thanks so much."

"Not at all," I said. "I'm happy to do it."

More than happy.

AFTER THE FUNERAL

I go to Storrs, Connecticut, to a little furnished room I have for my teaching stay each week. I can finally burst into sobs and realize Cal is gone forever. Living alone is painful and sometimes frightening. Having the companionship of Cal this past summer was a wonderful break of lightness and brightness for me.

When I return to Castine, Cal seems to be everywhere. His red flannel shirt and woolen socks are a painful discovery. His death is unacceptable, and yet I know he is gone, and it is very difficult to put the two things together.

THE ART OF LOSING

It's strange that the poem expressing my true state of mind, "One Art," is not written by Cal, but by his dear friend, Elizabeth Bishop. The form is a villanelle, a fixed verse of nineteen lines, five tercets followed by a quatrain. Elizabeth wrote sixteen drafts of the poem for her student and lover Alice Methfessel. It begins:

> The art of losing isn't hard to master;

She then goes on to list numerous lost objects, door keys, an heirloom watch, and then the more significant losses, her former houses and cities. She accepts all those loses with equanimity . . . until . . .

> —Even losing you (the joking voice, a gesture
> I love) I shan't have lied. It's evident
> The art of losing's not too hard to master
> Though it may look like (*Write it!*) like disaster.

I love that poem, so much so that I track down its first draft. It begins in what sounds like prose:

"One might begin by losing one's reading glasses, Oh, 2 or 3 times a day—or one's favorite pen."

I can visualize Elizabeth sitting at her desk, beginning with what is directly in front of her, then slowly in later drafts finding the true purpose of the poem . . . accepting the inevitability of loss. Like Samuel Beckett, "We are born astride of a grave, the light gleams an instant, then it's night once again." Ah, Beckett, that glorious depressive. "Down in the hole, lingeringly, the grave digger puts on the forceps." Language. It's all about language. The economy and the precision of the phrase . . . as if cut in stone.

Life passes in an instant. You begin dying the day you're born. Hard truth. But it's knowing that life is ephemeral that gives it value. Seize the day! And yet it is the curse of the writing class to live a virtual life. Even my darling extremist, Cal, said that he had a better time writing about his life than living it.

Where was I . . . before this digression, before all roads led to Cal. And to literature. That's how we curators of words understand our lives. We see the world through the quotes of others and count ourselves rich by our remembering.

Back to Elizabeth Bishop, her first draft's last paragraph:

"One might think this would have prepared me for losing one average sized, not exceptionally beautiful or dazzlingly intelligent person (except for the blue eyes). But it doesn't seem to, at all."

That's Alice, of course, who has left Elizabeth for someone younger and male. But in the end, in the final draft, Alice is anonymous, a shape-shifter for the reader's disastrous loss.

I prefer that privacy. I know when I write about others' lives, I'm writing about myself. But I prefer to be in shadows, discreet.

Cal pleads his case for the opposite in the last poem he writes, aptly titled "Epilogue."

> Yet why not say what happened?
> Pray for the grace of accuracy . . .
> We are poor passing facts,
> warned . . . to give
> each figure in the photograph
> his living name.

And that's what he did. Is it time for me to forgive?

ON LOSS AND LEAR: THREE ENDINGS

I am teaching *King Lear* to my Barnard writing students. You must know, I tell them, that Shakespeare borrowed his plots. No one minded. A judgment with which I concur, not being fond of plots myself. All narratives have been told before, it's what you bring to it that makes the story worth retelling.

"King Leir" was a legend, well known in Shakespeare's day, about an old king who decides to partition his kingdom to his three daughters, Goneril, Regan, and his youngest, Cordelia. He will determine the size of the gift based on each daughter's espousal of her love for him. The two older wax extravagantly about their endless loyalty and adoration. Cordelia's response is modest: she loves him in accordance with her duty, no more, no less. Incurring Leir's rage, he disinherits and banishes her. After the perfidy of the two older sisters, Cordelia and her husband come to Leir's aid and the three go on to rule the kingdom. Virtue is rewarded. An expected and happy ending.

In Shakespeare's *Lear* we find two versions. In the first version, the folio, the play ends with a stricken Lear carrying Cordelia's corpse. He moans

> No, no life
> Why should a dog, a horse, a rat have life
> And thou no breath at all?
> O, thou wilt come no more
> Never, never, never.
> Pray you, undo this button. O O O O!
> Break heart, I prithee, break.

That version was too brutal for the audience and Shakespeare tempered it, in the quarto, by allowing Lear to die with the false hope that Cordelia still may live:

> Never, never, never, never, never!
> Pray you undo this button. Thank you, sir.
> Do you see this? Look on her, look, her lips.
> Look there, look there.

Lear dies with that consolation; he has suffered enough.

Samuel Johnson voiced the dissatisfaction of many with Cordelia's death when he wrote:

"A play in which the wicked prosper, and the virtuous miscarry, may doubtless be good, because it is a just representation of the common events of human life. But since all reasonable beings naturally love justice the audience will be better pleased from the final triumph of persecuted virtue."

I dismiss the class without adding my own coda. Am I not Cordelia, modest, loyal, truth-telling? Does not my virtue deserve the reward of justice? Would not the audience walk away feeling better?

A SINGLE WOMAN

I am sixty. Mary McCarthy tells me it's still a marriageable age and demonstrates it herself by leaving her third husband, Bowden Broadwater, to marry James West, a career diplomat. Everyone knew Bowden was a homosexual, despite Mary insisting that he was merely "light on his feet."

She calls James West the first real man she has married. He is strong, handsome, and devoted. They have an elegant apartment in Paris, another in New York, and a large home for summer entertaining in Castine.

I am not interested in marrying again or even in having an affair. I want peace and autonomy. I intend to spend the next stage of my life with my writing, my daughter, and my women friends.

When asked, had I known what I was getting into, would I have married Cal?

The breakdowns were not the whole story. He was the best thing that ever happened to me.

ADVANCE OBITUARIES

There is a Society of Professional Obituary Writers. They meet annually and give out trophies, "Grimmies" shaped like tombstones, for best short obituary, best long obituary, and my personal favorite . . . lifetime achievement.

In the case of well- known people, their obituaries are written beforehand and kept on file. Occasionally they are published by error while the subject is still alive, which can be an embarrassment. Although, every once in a while, it can be felicitous.

In 1888, several newspapers announced Alfred Nobel's passing, in a mix-up related to his brother Ludwig's death. A French newspaper, in its obit on the Swedish arms manufacturer, thundered, "The merchant of death is dead. He became rich, through the invention of dynamite, to find ways to kill more people faster than ever before."

On reading the report, Nobel is said to have become

distressed about how the world would remember him. It led to him bequeathing the bulk of his estate to form the Nobel Prize.

MY OBIT

I suspect it has already been written for the *New York Times* and is simply waiting for the proper date to be affixed.

ELIZABETH HARDWICK, RESTLESS WOMAN OF LETTERS, DIES

Elizabeth Hardwick, who as a studious Kentucky belle set her ambitions on becoming a member of New York's glittering intellectual elite and then achieved them, as a critic, essayist, fiction writer and co-founder of the *New York Review of Books*, died yesterday in Manhattan. She was ???? years of age. Her death was confirmed by her daughter, Harriet Lowell.

Ms. Hardwick was among the last of an era of rambunctious intellectuals that included Edmund Wilson, Mary McCarthy, Phillip Rahv, and Robert Lowell, with whom she had a publicly turbulent marriage.

I prefer the following:

Hardwick, Elizabeth: The American Academy of Arts and

Lynne Kaufman

Letters notes with sorrow the death of our esteemed colleague. To plant a Memorial Tree, please visit our Sympathy Store.

POSTSCRIPT

This diary has served its purpose. I am ready to destroy it. And then I remember Cal's plea during the worst days of our separation. "Whatever you do, don't burn your Notebook! I hope to live in it long after I'm dirt."

ACKNOWLEDGMENTS

I am appreciative of the information and insights gained from the following:

Bishop, Elizabeth. "One Art," *The Complete Poems 1927-1979*. Farrar, Straus, and Giroux, 1983.

Brightman, Carol. *Writing Dangerously: Mary McCarthy and her World*. Random House, 1992.

Arendt, Hannah and Mary McCarthy. *Between Friends: The Correspondence of Hannah Arendt and Mary McCarthy 1949-1975*, edited by Carol Brightman. Harcourt, Brace and Company, 1995.

Hamilton, Ian. *Robert Lowell: A Biography*. Random House, 1982.

Hardwick, Elizabeth. *Seduction and Betrayal: Women and Literature*. 1974. NYRB Classics, 2001.

Sleepless Nights. 1979. NYRB Classics, 2011.

"Elizabeth Hardwick: The Art of Fiction LXXVII." Interview by Darryl Pinckney. *The Paris Review*, Summer 1985, #96.

Hardwick, Elizabeth and Robert Lowell. *The Dolphin Letters, 1970-1979*, edited by Saskia Hamilton. Farrar, Straus, and Giroux, 2019.

Jamison, Redford Kay. *Robert Lowell: Setting the River on Fire*. Vintage Books, 2017.

Kiernan, Frances. *Seeing Mary Plain: A life of Mary McCarthy*. W.W. Norton and Company, 2000.

Laskin, David. *Partisans*. Simon and Schuster, 2000.

Lowell, Robert. *The Dolphin*. Faber, 1973.

Mariani, Paul. *Lost Puritan: A Life of Robert Lowell*. W.W. Norton and Company, 1994.

Myers, Jeffrey. *Robert Lowell in Love*. University of Massachusetts Press, 2016.

ABOUT THE AUTHOR

LYNNE KAUFMAN is the author of three novels (*Slow Hands*, *Wild Women's Weekend*, and *Taking Flight*). Her short stories have been published in *McCall's*, *Redbook*, and *Cosmopolitan*. An accomplished playwright whose award-winning works have been produced across the country, Ms. Kaufman has degrees from Hunter College and Columbia University and now teaches writing at the Fromm Institute at the University of San Francisco and the Osher Lifelong Learning Institute at San Francisco State University. She is married with two adult children.

www.ingramcontent.com/pod-product-compliance
Lightning Source LLC
LaVergne TN
LVHW041919070526
838199LV00051BA/2672